THE FOLLOWERS

This is a work of fiction. All of the characters, organizations, and events portrayed in this novel are either products of the authors' imaginations or are used fictitiously.

ISBN 978-0-692-83101-4

Acknowledgements:

Thank you Craig for always believing in my pipe dreams.

Thank you to Becky Mirro for giving me back my inspiration, and Kristi Stark for help with editing and helping me stay sane.

This book may be Purchased for educational, business or promotional use. For information on bulk purchases, please contact nursecamelot@aol.com

THE FUNERAL

Rain drizzled down, as the black limousine rolled down the long drive. The two-story mansion sat on a vast property of Grand Old Oaks, Spanish moss slowly swayed in the cold wet breeze. Inside, the housekeepers and cooks scurried about.

Mark stood at the bottom of the staircase. He was a large man, big shouldered, square jawed. His hair was cropped short in a military style, and the darkness of it offset his piercing blue eyes. He wore a black pin-striped suit and a black leather duster, hiding his holstered weapon.

His mind drifted back to the first time he entered this house. Driving up, he had wondered what kind of man Jack Goldberg really was. Did he have a soul and integrity...Or would he be like all of the other rich and arrogant pricks that ran the Earth?

To his surprise, Jack answered the door personally, and warmly shook his hand, leading him to the Library. "Please sit down" he had said, pointing to one of the two large over-stuffed leather chairs. They sat and made small talk for a while. Jack showed Mark the layout of the house and grounds, and gave him a rundown on the new high-tech security system he had recently installed. Mark asked Jack, why he needed protection to such an extent. "I've become a rich man, and there are always threats, but it's not me you'll be protecting. It's my daughter." Mark distinctly remembered shaking his head and telling Jack, "I don't guard children." He didn't like kids. He didn't even know how to deal with them.

Jack had assured him that at seventeen, she was hardly a child. She had graduated early and would start college in the fall.

He distinctly remembered saying "no." Yet here he stood, six years later, waiting for Megan to come downstairs, so they could say goodbye to the only family she had. Not to mention, the only man that he had ever respected and cared for.

Mark had led a solitary life. The son of a prostitute, he had never known his father. His mother, refused to talk about him, and at seventeen, when she died of a Heroin overdose, he joined the army.

The structure felt good to him, he thrived on it. He moved up quickly in the ranks and was easily promoted. Later, he joined an elite team, a team that only moved in the shadows and didn't exist. After watching his men die at the hands of a foreign enemy, he had sought his revenge and once again joined the world.

He began working security, and soon made a name for himself. He hated every minute of it; the spoiled rich men that hired him, and their cheap wives that propositioned him more than once. He preferred his own company, and didn't trust anyone.

That was until he met Jack Goldberg. He liked his mannerism and the warmth in his eyes- it put him at ease, which was a new feeling for him. Over the years, their relationship had grown into a true kinship, much more than a job.

He ran his hand through his hair, dreading the funeral, and the days to come. Mark sat on the last step of the staircase, waiting patiently for Megan.

She took one last look in the mirror, her sad eyes staring back at her. Megan thought about the last few days, all of the added security made her nervous. She didn't know what had gotten into her father.

 He had acted so strange in the last weeks before his death. Every day he was adding new things to their security. He became almost manic about it she had brought the subject up several dozen times, only to hear her father say the same thing, that he was a "rich man who was concerned for her safety as well as his own." Although she never felt he was telling her everything, trying to sway her father had always been an impossible thing.

Megan had joined her father's firm when she turned twenty one, and turned out to be more of a work-horse than Jack. She enjoyed the job, it kept her mind occupied. Megan was five foot two and a hundred pounds at best.

Her long brown hair hung to her waist, and although she was small she could outwork, and outlast the best men in her father's firm. She had her father's drive, and his head for business.

Jack had been a self-made man, orphaned by his parents at a young age. He worked his way from job to job, eventually landing a position in a real estate firm. Jack learned about property, and over the course of a few years, he purchased a rental here and there, and eventually opened his own firm. By the time he married Anita, Megan's mother, his business was well established. They were introduced by a congressman to whom Jack had sold a house. Their courtship was a whirlwind, they did everything together.

They would laugh and talk for hours into the night, always inseparable. He loved watching her. She had soft blonde hair, and blue eyes. Anita laughed and sang at home and in the garden.

They dreamed of a family and a future. In public, she was quiet and sullen even. His friends considered her a gold-digger. But Jack didn't care about that. He had met her in July, they were married by August, and a month later she was pregnant. He was ecstatic. He loved her beyond belief.

Suddenly everything had changed. She stopped talking, stopped laughing. She disappeared for hours at a time. He worried for her and the baby.

Jack tried to give her the space she needed and chalked it up to her pregnancy and hormones. He hoped that once the baby came, they would be happy again.

The week before Megan was born, Anita had moved into the guest room. She looked thin, her eyes had become dull. She had dark circles under them and did not look like the woman he had met only a few short months ago.

He didn't understand. Everything had changed. When he tried to talk to her, she walked away. Once the baby was born, he planned to get Anita checked out by all of the best Doctors, and rebuild their relationship.

He came home early and found her in the attic, in a situation that he would not speak of again until years later.

That was really the beginning of the end. Jack hired a private detective, and found out that Anita was an esteemed member of the divine Rainbow, A cult that she had been adopted into.

Her parents and grandparents had been members. His hopes of reconciliation and a normal marriage and family would never come to pass.

The night Anita and Megan came home from the hospital, he had given the cook the night off and was making a romantic dinner. The last ditch effort to save what was already lost.

He walked upstairs to wake Anita, and to his shock she was gone. The baby was sound asleep in her crib. On the nightstand, he found a note that read, "Jack, I can't do this. Don't try to follow me. I don't love you. I never did."

Frantically, he searched the house and property. The old Buick that she had, when they met was gone. He ran back upstairs, picked up Megan and held her close, tears flowing down his face. His heart hurt, not only because she left him, but, how could she leave her own child.

It was unfathomable to him. Easing down into his grandmother's old rocking chair, he shook his head, and rocked the baby back to sleep.

Jack did the best he could and after a few days, he hired a Nanny, and life went on. Somehow He got through each day. He carried on, with shaky legs, because of Megan, and eventually his heart mended, although there was never another woman in his life.

Jack preferred it that way. He was handsome and rich, but he never got over the shock of having his wife walk out on him and the baby. He could never go through pain like that again. He devoted his life to his business and his daughter.

The ride to the graveyard was long and uncomfortable. Megan stood stone faced, as she had through the entire service. Her heart pounded in her chest. She starred at her shoes. Her Father had been her whole life.

She couldn't believe the events of the last few days. Finding her father dead, now here they were saying goodbye. It seemed surreal. Like a bad dream.

There had been hundreds of people at Jacks service, but since the hard rain had started, the crowd had dissipated. Now it was just her, Mark and the priest.

Father Pat finished his last words, and they shook hands saying their goodbyes. Mark stood next to Megan and held an umbrella over them both.

When she swayed, he steadied her. She looked thin and frail. A deep ache settled in his jaw. He realized he was clenching his teeth.

It was hard for him too. Mark felt an unfamiliar lump in his throat. He was unaccustomed to sorrow. He kept a safe distance his entire life, but Jack had been much more than his employer. He was his only friend.

Megan squeezed his hand in desperation. He swallowed hard and choked back the tears. Her hand felt warm in his. He had to stay strong. He was all she had now. He had a job to do.

He had sworn an oath to Jack. His mind wandered to the first few years. Mark thought back to all the times Megan had resented him tagging along, ruining her life, as she had told him countless times.

The few dates she had, had ended quickly and awkwardly. Most teenage boys didn't appreciate a six foot two body guard in the back seat.

Mark scanned the tree line. He saw Anita, and two men standing at the edge of the woods. He knew she would come. It was only a matter of time, like a rat out of the sewer. Now he had to tell Megan the truth. He starred at her, and un-holstered his weapon.

The reading of the will would be tomorrow and he knew she would be there. Megan squeezed his hand, and said "I want to go home." Tears streamed down her face. She made no attempt to wipe them. He pulled out a handkerchief and handed it to her.

They walked to the limousine. The driver opened the door and they got into the back. Stan started the engine, and they eased out of the graveyard.

Mark glanced back at the wood line, Anita and the two men were gone. He knew it wasn't for long.

He thought back to the last conversation he had had with Jack. It was the night before he had died. Jack had summoned him to the library. He had paced the room, "The time we prepared for is here. I need you to follow the instructions exactly the way we planned. He wouldn't go into greater detail. He just wanted the ball to start rolling and said they would talk more in the next few days.

Mark attempted to press him, but Jack seemed distracted, and avoided any further conversation.

Mark knew Anita had paid him a visit, at the office, but Jack alluded to the conversation.

There must have been something else, something he didn't tell him. Mark knew about the cult. Jack had been open about that since early on. But this new secrecy had Mark on edge.

Megan had been leaning on him on the drive. Suddenly she sat up and straightened her hair that had blown in the storm. Her shoulders squared. She took a deep breath and sat up straighter. It was in this moment that he knew she was her father's daughter, and that she would weather this storm.

Mark knew the biggest storm of all was on its way.

They rode in silence. His mind continued to wander. He thought of Jack, his warmth, how he had made him feel like he was part of something more. His eyes misted over. The lump in his throat hurt.

He looked over at Megan and their eyes met. She took his hand and gave it a gentle squeeze. "We're going to be ok." She said. Mark shook his head, and swallowed hard. "I know." He replied. But in reality he knew that was the farthest thing from the truth.

Jack had told him, "You keep her alive, no matter what you have to do. If things go south, you take the money and the envelope." Jack had planned for them all to go. It was as if Jack had known he would not be making the trip.

Now Mark was left holding the bag. He knew the hardest part would be explaining it all to Megan, and telling her that her father's death was no accident.

He had seen the two small puncture wounds in Jacks neck. His contact at the FBI would confirm it. The worst part was that the bastards had been in the house. That pissed him off. Megan had grown up in that house. It was their sanctuary. Now, even that wasn't safe.

He knew that Jack didn't always arm the security system until Megan came home. That night they had arrived after ten. Megan had a late meeting had insisted on eating Chinese food in town.

When they arrived it was almost midnight, and they both assumed Jack had retired for the night. Mark had armed the security system himself, shaking his head, and making a mental note to tell Jack about it.

Everything had looked fine. The guards were in place. Nothing looked out of the ordinary.

To someone on the outside all the security seemed excessive. Jack was a real estate tycoon, so to speak, not a politician or royalty.

Jack had told Mark the secret of the night he had come home to find her in the attic, chanting with a pentagram and candles, and six others. Jack had seen strange markings were drawn on her pregnant belly. He went into a rage, screaming and chasing everyone out. Anita had laughed in his face.

He had done research on the Cult after Mark had come along. They had become well established and organized in the last two decades. Their roots ran far into the political scene, deep into old southern money. This cult was rising quickly, and would grow to be to be one of the most powerful.

Morning came quickly. Mark sat at the small table in the kitchen. He was on his third cup of coffee, when Megan came in.

Fred the groundskeeper came in behind her. He had been employed by Jack for over twenty years, he wasn't much help anymore but Jack had insisted he stay on, more to help Fred, than anything else.

Jack had had a way of making people feel important. He had a few old timers running around, they continued on the payroll. He felt obligated to keep them on.

"There's someone at the front gate to see Miss Megan," Fred said. Mark handed Megan a cup of coffee, as they walked to the security room to look at the cameras. There she was on the screen, with the same two men, that Mark had seen at the funeral.

"I don't believe it, my long lost mother." Megan said. "I didn't know, you knew her," Mark replied. "I recognize her from a photo my father showed me last year."

She leaned in closer to get a better look at Anita. Mark pushed the intercom to the front Gate. "What do you want?" "I want to talk to Megan."

"Get lost". Mark replied.

"Wait," Megan said. "I want to hear what she has to say."

She pushed the button. "What do you want?" Megan asked. "I've come for what's rightfully mine." She replied. "I'm Jacks widow, I'm entitled to everything." "Wrong," Megan replied, "You are entitled to nothing. Goodbye Anita."

She set down the microphone and walked back to the kitchen. Mark watched as the two men talked to Anita.

She stood like a stone starring towards the house, with a faint smile. It was eerie. He had seen some crazy shit in his day, but she was another story. She stood there for a good ten minutes, as if in a trance. Then suddenly she walked away, the men following behind her. Mark sighed, and shook his head.

He joined Megan in the kitchen. The silence was obvious. Mark made pancakes with bacon and they both ate without speaking. "That Bitch," Megan finally said.

"My father isn't even cold yet and here she is to cash in. She must have missed the memo about the divorce." She stabbed at her pancakes in a rage. "Do you know he only divorced her two years ago? Two!!!!! I told him and told him, that he should just do it. I don't know why he didn't." She shook her head in disgust.

"Will you go with me to the reading tomorrow?" She asked. She handed him her plate and he set them in the sink.

"Megan, we need to talk about that." He replied. She walked over to him. "I really need a hug." Before he knew it she was standing right in front of him.

He put his arms around her carefully. She hugged him tightly burying her face in his chest. The entire gesture took him by surprise.

He was embarrassed that he noticed the fragrant smell of her hair, her perfume, and the way she felt in his arms.

He knew she wasn't a child, but he had never thought of her as a woman. He stepped back awkwardly, and sighed. "There are things you need to know."

"What things?" "About your parents, things your father didn't tell you."

"Like what?" She eyed him suspiciously. "What do you remember about your mother?" "Nothing much, bits and pieces my dad told me over the years. I don't have any real memories I was a baby when she left."

Mark ran his hand through his hair. He was nervous. "Do you know why she left?" "I don't know Mark, because she was a bitch?" Her voice was loud and irritated now.

"No," he said calmly. "Your mother fell in with some questionable people."

"Questionable People? WHAT DOES THAT MEAN?" To her he was talking in circles, like her father. "Your mother became part of a cult."

She starred at him dumbfounded. "What the hell do you mean?" "Even before they met, she had become part of this cult. While she was pregnant with you her behavior changed, she became distant, erratic even.

Your father came home early one night and found them in the attic. Her and other members, they were performing some ritual. Your father threw them out and laid the law down to her that it would never happen again. Anita laughed in his face, and after that day things were never the same. She became more distant. Then after you were born she just left.

He hired a private investigator a few years ago, and found out the cult has really become massive. There are thousands of members. It is a very large operation.

Anita disappeared off the radar, and he didn't hear from her again until two weeks ago. She showed up at the office and said she was here for you, and that it was time for you to take your rightful place in the cult."

Mark didn't mention that Jack had omitted all this information, and that he had obtained it from a surveillance tape.

"He didn't tell me what else was said between them, but it was enough for him to put security on high alert. He was scared. I've never seen him like that. He looked like he saw a ghost."

"Do you think I'm in danger?" Megan asked. "Yes, they have been casing the house and they were at the funeral watching.

I don't like it. I've done some research on them too they are dangerous and they have wide reach."

He knew Jack's death wasn't an accident, but she had enough to absorb. Mark wasn't ready to tell her and she wasn't ready to hear it.

"We'll call the police." She said in a matter of fact tone. "No Megan, we can't call the police. I told you they have a wide grasp. I have no idea who is involved. Right now we can't trust anyone. We need to get out of here for a while."

He paced back and forth.

"That's what your Dad had planned. We were all supposed to go. Now it's just us. Things have changed. After the will is read all bets are off. She still thinks she stands to inherit something, maybe everything, and the cult is too greedy to give that up.

Once she finds out that there is nothing, they will come, full force."

"I'm not running away, I have a life here". She stated loudly.

"We aren't running. We are leaving for a while, until I can get a handle on this and find out what's going on, and who is involved. I can't protect you here. Your father left strict instructions. The business will continue on, you can call Art in the morning, he can fax you all the papers. We won't be at the reading of the will. Your father left this key."

He handed her a small silver key. "It's to a safety deposit box. To be opened only by you in the event of his death. I will take you tomorrow morning." Megan took the key out of his hand gently. Her mind was reeling.

"This is really serious isn't it?" He sighed.

"Yes honey it is I'm sorry." He patted her shoulder lightly. "We leave tomorrow morning. I'm going to drive you to the bank and to the country club like every Friday. They have been watching us, and I've been watching them. You will go into the bank, like you always do. Get as much cash as you can, and the safety deposit box.

Then I will drop you off at the club. You'll go in and head straight through to the back service entrance. I will be there in a white van with tinted windows. Don't come out until you see my face." She starred at him for a moment.

"This is really crazy isn't it? How do you know they won't try to grab me at the club?"

"They won't," he said. "You know how we have been going out to the point for ice cream every Friday after the club?" "Yes." She twirled her hair, a nervous gesture she had done since childhood.

"That is the most secluded spot. That's where they will make their move. Except we won't be there.

We will be long gone by the time they figure out what happened."

She sighed, and shook her head. Her long hair framed her face. He could tell she was scared. Mark put his hand on her shoulders and gave her another reassuring squeeze. "It's gonna be ok. Pack your bags and put them in the hall. I'll pick them up and load the car tonight. Then in the morning we'll go".

He watched her turn without saying a word and run up the steps two at a time. He hated that it had to be this way, but in his gut he knew that they were running out of time.

Mark walked the house. He checked all the doors and windows. He loaded the other shotgun and 9mm. His other weapons and ammo were already packed.

Much later Mark spoke to the guards and put them on high alert. He watched them, one by one. A guard had let an intruder into the house. Of that he was sure. He wished he knew which one. The rage he felt was hard to contain.

Mark couldn't remember crying or feeling sad, or much of anything. When Jack had been killed, his feelings had been overwhelming. Now he turned it to rage. A cold collected rage that could wait its turn.

He doubled the guards at the gate, and had four in the courtyard, and around the perimeter of the house. Old guards paired with new guards.

He was sure they would try to grab her tomorrow, but he had to make provisions in case he was wrong.

He checked the doors and windows one more time.

He didn't like the idea of her being upstairs, but knowing it was safe for now, Mark entered the small guest room off of the kitchen. He had moved into it, when Jack started adding new security. The room had housed the cook for years.

It was a small white room, with a single bed. He had a simple black satin bedspread. He would have never told anyone, but he liked the way it felt against his skin. It was one of the few luxuries he afforded himself. A silver lamp sat in the corner, on the wall a picture of a tree and a field. Simple, the way he liked it.

He showered quickly, slipped on his grey sweats, and lay down on the bed with his arms folded behind his head. He started to drift off to sleep when he heard a soft knock.

Mark was on his feet, the 40 caliber in his hand. He opened the door, to see Megan with her pillow and blanket.

"I'm scared." She said quietly. He opened the door, to let her pass. He grabbed his pillow and blanket off the bed. "Here , you can sleep... here. I'll take the floor."

Megan didn't argue. She got into bed, and thirty minutes later as he lay on the floor, he could hear her breathing change. She was asleep. He was glad she had come down. It worried him, her being upstairs alone. After all Jack had been killed in this very house. He felt responsible for not being there.

Mark thought over the plans for the tomorrow one more time. It was his job to keep her alive. He hoped he could pull it all off without a hitch.

Her breathing was distracting him. Mark was getting pissed at himself. He had to think clearly. He could smell her shampoo. Earlier, he had smelled it, in the kitchen when she had insisted on hugging him.

He closed his eyes, and breathed it in. His thoughts drifted. Catching himself he sighed. There wasn't time for such foolishness.

He had to go over everything one more time. Tomorrow would proceed like any other day, and the key would be to stay calm, to keep Megan calm, and not to attract any unwanted attention.

The other vehicle that they would need had already been dropped off. Mark had made the first set of preparations that he and Jack had agreed upon.

He still had some connections. If it all went well, it would be a miracle.

Megan mumbled in her sleep and rolled over. He was instantly distracted thinking of the way she smelled again.

He closed his eyes, and said a prayer that all would go well. Hours later, sleep finally came. The night passed quickly. When Mark opened his eyes the sun was already coming up.

He showered, dressed and made coffee. Mark had loaded the bags and was on his third cup of coffee, when Megan came into the room. "Hi," she said sleepily.

"Hey, how did you sleep?" "Good, I feel a little more rested than yesterday." She pulled her hair up and tied it in a makeshift knot.

"What about you? You look tired." "I'm alright." He lied, handing her a cup of coffee. She smiled at him. It was a faint scared smile. "I guess I'll go get ready." She said, as she headed towards the large marble staircase.

"I have things to do." He stated and walked away, avoiding the conversation. He had to keep to the business at hand. Since first light he had patrolled the house and grounds, checking every detail. He felt wired, nervous even, which was unusual for him.

Normally, he was composed and ready to do the job, with little thought, of himself or anyone.

There had been times that he had prayed for death, to be killed in the line of duty. Those were dark lonely times. Times, when he had tired, of being alone and performing the same meaningless job day after day for people, that didn't even deserve the things they had.

Now things had changed. He felt more alive today than he had in a long time, and although he had loved Jack, this was different. The monotony of the last five years was gone and he had a distinct purpose.

It was going to be a long day. He didn't trust the guards. Some were new and he didn't know them well. Some had been around for decades, he trusted them even less. He knew the cult had a wide reach, and anyone could be a part of it.

His gut told him that today would be the day, and once they left the safety of the house, all bets would be off.

Megan dialed Art's number and he answered right away. He was a short little man, with grey hair that never seemed to lay right. He always looked a little disheveled. Art told her he was sorry for her loss. He had been her father's attorney for as long as she could remember.

She felt a little annoyed that Mark didn't want her to tell him the truth. She sat down on the marble bench, at the base of the stairs. Her hair was pulled into a tight bun. Megan wore jeans, and a black tank top, covered by a loose pink sweater. She narrowed her eyes at Mark. "Art, I won't be able to come to the reading today, I'm just so upset, I think I will just hang around the house." She trusted him, and gave Mark an annoyed look, until he looked away. "That's fine Megan. Will you be there all day?"

"I'm probably going to the club later, and to the bank."

"I was just wondering. I will fax all the papers over to you. All you have to do is sign them, and fax them back to me. Will Mark be staying on with you then?"

"Yes."

"That's good. Your dad would have wanted it that way." He replied.

"I hope you will stay too." She hinted.

"You know I will." He said kindly.

Minutes later the papers were on the Fax. Megan signed them and faxed them back.

Jack had left her the company and the house, and most of his land, all the properties, and bank accounts. He had left a nice nest egg for Mark, and several properties.

Megan got up from the bench. She crossed the room to where Mark stood. She looked down and gently took his large hand in hers.

"I'm so scared. I don't know what's going to happen."

He looked her in the eyes. "Megan, hear me when I tell you, you are safe with me."

"You want me to just jump into a car with you, and run off to god knows where, with a bunch of crazy people chasing us." She was escalating rather quickly. He touched her lightly on the shoulder, "Megan, you know me. I'm doing what's best for you right now. I need to take you somewhere where I can keep you safe." He knew there wasn't time for this right now.

"I'm not going anywhere until you tell me everything you know." He was getting irritated. She could be the most annoying woman on the face of the planet.

"Look, there are people that want to kidnap you, and worse. We need to go, and we need to DO IT NOW." He realized he was getting loud, he closed his eyes, and lowered his voice. "I'm sorry, I don't mean to yell. Please, Megan, trust me now. I would never do anything to hurt you. I'm only trying to keep you safe, and get you somewhere where we can figure out our next move. Now, get your bag, and lets go. I will tell you everything I know, soon." He grabbed her shoulders and steered her toward the door.

They drove out of the gate onto the street. The dark sedan that was parked across the street followed. Mark drove the same route, he did every Friday. When he pulled into the bank parking lot, the other car pulled in a few spaces behind him and parked.

It annoyed him that they seriously thought that they weren't seen, or that he hadn't noticed them following him for weeks.

"Aren't you coming with me?" Megan said anxiously. "No, I don't usually come in we have to act like we always do." "This isn't the place."

Megan shook her head and went into the bank alone. He wasn't worried about the bank. There was one way in, one way out. The bank would draw too much attention.

Megan came out a few minutes later. "I emptied the safety deposit box, and got some money out of savings. Do you think $500,000 will be enough?"

"Jesus Christ, I didn't mean the whole bank."

"Well I don't know where we are going, or how long we will be gone." She replied defensively. After slamming her door, she yanked her seatbelt on and starred out the window.

He didn't like the way things were going. Her attitude could be dangerous for them both.

Twenty minutes later they pulled up in front of the country club. The car still close behind, pulled onto the edge of the parking lot. He could make out two men through the dark windows.

"Take your racket, and your bag, there is a gun in your bag, In case you need it."

"Oh MY GOD," He knew the look of panic. She breathed heavily. She was on the verge of hyperventilating.

"Megan," He grabbed her hands and held them tightly. "Look at me." Their eyes met, hers wide with fear. He spoke quietly now.

"This is not going to be the place. This is the last thing you have to do today. Take your bag. Go inside. Go to the bathroom." He spoke slowly, but deliberately.

"In ten minutes, come out the back service entrance. I will be in a white van, with tinted windows. I will roll the window down. As soon as you see me, come out and get into the van. That's it. You are going to be ok. Breathe.

"I'm so scared." Her eyes were tearing up.

Mark knew time was of the essence.

"I'm sorry, I know you're scared, but you need to get out of the car....Now. You can do this. I know you can." He let go of her hands, and she exited the car.

She waved to him as she did every time, trying to fake a smile. Her heart pounded, and her palms were sweating. As soon as he saw she was safely inside he drove away, as he did every week. Mark drove past the dark sedan that had been joined by a second. Except today he didn't run errands.

He prayed he was right. He didn't like leaving her alone, but all his years of training told him this was not the place. They wouldn't expect him back for two hours, then, they would follow them to the secluded beach and try to kill him and grab Megan.

He had picked the beach over a month ago. It was easy to talk Megan into Ice cream. It soon became a Friday ritual, just as he had hoped.

Mark knew they would like the seclusion of the beach road, and would make their plan accordingly. It was all part of the master plan.

Mark headed down the highway. No one was behind him. He wasn't the target. Driving around to the next Block, he parked the car, and waited to make sure no one had followed. Mark exited the Car, and transferred the bags to the white service van. He drove back to the club and pulled around the Back.

 The two dark sedans sat in the same place where he had left them, with a third pulling in. He inched his way up to the service door and rolled down the window. Megan came out, and got into the van. "OH my god, I was about to have a nervous breakdown."

 "Get down". He instructed her, pulling the baseball cap down over his face, so he wouldn't be recognized.

He eased the van through the parking lot, right past the three cars. He couldn't help but smile. Picturing their faces, when they realized they had missed their Target.

He figured Anita would already be furious after the reading of the will, since she didn't know Jack had ever filed for divorce. It was a nice little surprise Jack had left behind for her. Anything was possible with money.

This would set her over the top. At least one of the men out in the cars would surely lose their Nuts today. He smiled at the thought.

"See? Everything is ok" he told Megan. He pulled the hat off, and smiled. She eyed him suspiciously.

 "What are you smiling about?"

"Nothing", he replied. They aren't going to know we are gone for two hours.

Jack would be so proud.

ANITA

Anita watched the three black sedans pull into the driveway. She walked out to meet them. The men exited the cars. No one spoke. Anita starred them, looking from face to face.

No one made eye contact. "Where is she?" She spat.

"Ma'am she never came out of the club." John and Paul hung their heads. They hated when she was angry. There was no telling what she would do.

She had been beside herself after she came out of the lawyers Office, screaming and ripping out her hair in the back of the car. "Did you go inside?" Anita's eyes were bulging.

"YES, she wasn't there." The men hung their heads.

"Did anything unusual happen?"

"No, they left the house, went to the bank, then she went into the club. He never came back."

Anita turned and began to walk towards the house. She hated stupidity. She waved the other four men on. Paul and John followed her. Anita wore a peasant blouse and a red skirt. The skirt made a swishing noise as she stomped through the yard.

She could feel her blood boiling. They had missed her again. The last time she was supposed to be there, but instead Jack was waiting for them. She had been impressed. He still had his connections. Someone had tipped him off.

"Ok let me get this straight," She said, sitting down on the small chaise, smoothing her skirt.

"Megan never came out."

"Yes Ma'am," Paul answered. He was a small wiry man. Dark curly hair, he was of Italian descent and sported a thick accent. "Did we get his name, this guard of hers?" "No, we are working on it." John replied.

"You're working on it? That's what you have been saying for weeks. He's been a thorn in my side for a long while now. Did anyone check the house?" She was pacing now, her small, thin frame, moving quickly.

"MAYBE YOU MISSED HER, MAYBE SHE GOT A RIDE. MAYBE THE GUARD BROKE DOWN. MAYBE, MAYBE ,MAYBE ,IT'S BEEN HOURS AND NOONE THOUGHT TO CHECK THE FUCKING HOUSE?" she was screaming hysterically now. "We have a car heading there now."

"Well whose bright idea was that?" She asked them both.

"It was Paul's idea." John replied. "Well, at least someone here has a brain." She stated as she turned and shot John in the head. "Clean this mess up you fuck. I don't want blood on my carpet." She stepped over him.

"Where is Nathan?" She yelled as she stormed up the stairs. "I'm here", He replied. She entered the bedroom.

A single bed graced the room, as well as a small dresser filled with a dozen black robes. The furniture black as well, just like the walls.

Nathan was an Albino. He was light sensitive and had piercing pink eyes. He was one of a kind. At six foot eight, and two-Hundred and seventy pounds of muscle, he was a force to be reckoned with.

Anita had found him in the Streets, beaten left for dead. She had brought him home and nursed him back to health, and converted him to the cult in the process. She had molded him, and created him. His life was dedicated to Anita.

"I need you. I am angry." She stated. Her eyes glazed over with madness. "Nathan crossed the room, and pulled off his robe. He stood naked before her.

He was completely hairless, and had a back full of scars. His manhood stood proudly. He was well proportioned to say the least.

She turned and bent over the bed. He ripped her skirt up and tore her panties from her body. "Do it." She commanded. He entered her hard, and began to pound into her as she chanted.

THE ROAD

Mark headed up the Ramp to I-75 north toward Georgia. Megan had been silent for a while. He didn't press the issue.

He stopped at the first rest area as planned. "Why are we stopping?" Megan asked.

"We are changing cars." He replied as he parked the service van. After looking around he exited the van and opened the trunk to the Jeep Cherokee. He transferred the bags to the Jeep.

Mark escorted Megan into the rest area, to use the bathroom at her insistence. He rushed her out, and once back in the truck he veered onto the highway.

"You promised to tell me everything." She said quietly.

"Yes, I did." He replied. He ran his hand through his hair.

"Well I told you about the cult. Your father researched them through the years. They have grown much larger and have more members. It's a huge operation and they have a long reach. Some of the members are powerful prominent people. It's nothing to play with.

He and I did some research recently. There was a breach at the office and the front gate was tampered with. Some files went missing.

The gate code was tampered with at the house, and two guard uniforms went missing. Just little things, that wouldn't look like much to the average person. But it put us both on edge. That's when your dad started adding the extra security."

"They were reaching their feelers out, Looking for a weakness, looking to get in."

He drove on, glancing her way periodically.

"Then two weeks ago Anita came to your Dads office. She told him it was time for you to take your place in the group, that it's tradition. He threw her out. After that he was in panic mode."

Mark felt his face turning red. It all sounded so farfetched. Megan was staring at him like he was crazy. This would have sounded better coming from Jack.

Megan reached into her purse and pulled out her cell phone. "I'm just going to call the police." The color had drained from her face. "I can't do this."

"Well there's no battery. I took it out. Your phone is traceable. The police can't help us." He pulled the truck off the highway and slammed it into park.

"Don't you think you're dad already went to the police? This is a Cult we are dealing with. These are not small players. You don't say no to them. No one does. Anyone that crosses them ends up dead. Anita has been building this group since she left. You are a direct descendant of her bloodline and she will come for you."

She starred at him. "Who are these people? How will we know who is part of it?" she asked in dismay.

"There is no way to know. There is no one we can trust right now. That's what I've been trying to tell you."

They are called "The Divine Rainbow", They believe that Jesus is the antichrist, and that all humans are fallen angels that have been hypnotized.

They believe that they are the awakened, the only ones who know the truth. That, only the most dedicated to the cause know this.

The cult descends right down the bloodline, from mother to daughter. In order to keep her power she has to produce a direct descendant. I'm not sure what happened then, that's what we were working on finding out.

She is the most powerful high priestess of this organization.

Anita wanted the house and the land to further the cause, but ultimately that's not what she is after. She wants you. Jack and I did all the research."

She was crying now.

"There is nowhere for me to hide they are going to find me aren't they?"

"No, they aren't. That's why we are leaving. I couldn't protect you there. I need more time to find out the rest and to get more names, we need to find some kind of glitch that we can use. There is a chink in every suit of armor."

"I'm sorry I doubted you." She wiped her eyes.

"Here I am giving you a hard time and acting like a brat, and all you were trying to do was protect me."

"It's ok."

"No it's not. I've been mad at you for years. I couldn't even get a date because of you." She threw her hands up in the air.

"Now I know why. I'm sorry Mark."

She wiped her nose with her sleeve. He turned and wrapped his arms around her, as she sobbed.

Mark stroked her hair. "Megan," he said in a soft voice,

"It's going to be alright. I will find a way to fix this." They stayed like this for a while.

Thirty minutes later they were back on the highway.

 Megan went to sleep.

Mark's mind wandered. She still surprised him. Sometimes he forgot that she was only 23, and that besides the office, she had no outside life.

He had realized it, when she said she had never had a date because of him. Megan had been seventeen when he signed up with Jack.

She wasn't your typical teenager. Jack had kept her busy, but secluded. She had grown up among grownups, and it was true, Mark had been there on every date.

It was probably shameful, but he had actually pulled his 9mm and showed it to a date that was getting too friendly. There had been nothing else.

Megan worked and passed her free time reading and riding horses on the property. She spent hours in the barn. The smell of the hay calmed her. It smelled like home.

On Fridays she went to the country club to walk the treadmill and listen to music. He was with her until her bedroom door closed at night.

She never snuck out or had the urge to party. It simply wasn't her. That was the life they lived.

He thought back to the night that Jack had told him Anita had returned.

He had been frantic. There must have been something else that happened, after the meeting. The way Jack had acted and the panic in his voice made it clear that he was concerned. Whatever it was, he had taken it to the grave.

It put Mark on edge. It was the first time in his life that he felt fear for the people he protected.

They rode in silence for hours. When Megan woke up, they made small talk.

They stopped at a small Café on the outside of Atlanta for lunch. It was a quaint little place with white lace curtains and blue booths. They ate and had coffee.

She eventually asked him about his life, before coming to them. He told her of his Mother, and his job with the army.

Mark talked of a few missions, but even now he found it hard to speak of such things.

There had been many operations that he didn't agree with. Missions that he questioned, privately. In their line of work you didn't question openly.

People who asked questions or disagreed often disappeared all together. By the time his team had been killed he was on the verge of leaving.

He had had enough, of the secrecy, and the covert operations handed down by a government that only cared about money. It was the same old story.

He was deep in thought, and her question startled him.

"Have you ever killed anyone?"

"There have been a few." He replied. He already didn't like where this was going. "Because you were protecting someone?"

"At times, and when it was ordered." He felt like he needed to come clean, so she would know who, and what he was.

Megan starred at him. He could feel it. He kept his eyes on the road. He didn't want to be judged. Not now. He had done enough judging for them both.

"You mean you killed someone because someone told you to?" "That's right. It was my job." He answered.

"Does that change how you feel about me?" he asked, then after he said it, he didn't understand why he had said it at all.

"I guess you had to do what you had to do." She replied. She didn't want to judge him. He was after all risking his life. He had no obligation to her.

They stopped and ate dinner, and then pulled into a motel for the night.

The lack of sleep was catching up with Mark. He unloaded the truck and wondered how things had gotten so crazy.

Mark kept up a good front for Megan, but he knew he was out of his element. He could deal with a third- world country, living for days in the bush.

Defusing Bombs, guarding people from terrorists, stalkers, you name it. But this enemy was faceless, nameless.

It smiled in your face. He had never dealt with a cult. He was surprised at how much it had grown over the years.

There had to be a way to infiltrate it. The key was the members. If he could obtain a list, and he knew there had to be one, THAT would be the answer.

Here he was, in the middle of a mess. In the beginning it was for the promise he had made to Jack. Now he knew it was more. ....much more. Tomorrow he would have to tell Megan that her father had been murdered.

He thought of the two small puncture wounds, and the call from his contact at the coroner's office.

According to the toxicology report Jack had enough amphetamines in his system to kill a horse.

He should have told her sooner, but considering all she had been through, first finding her father dead, then trying to get her out of the house, and trying to explain the cult and all its intricacies, it would have been too much.

Now they were on the road and she had never been away from home.

He just wanted her to have a day to mourn before he broke the worst news of all to her.

They were in Chattanooga, Tennessee for the night. He figured he had put enough distance between them and Anita for one night. He brought in the last of the bags.

The motel was small and ratchet as Megan had stated. She was curled up on the bed fast asleep.

Tomorrow, they would head west toward the mountains, but for tonight this flea bag motel would do.

Mark thought of the cabin that was left to him by a friend. It was small but quaint and would provide safety and shelter for a while. It wasn't the Ritz Carleton but it would give him a chance to regroup and figure out his next move.

He locked the door and pulled the curtain closed. Mark took a quick shower, and grabbed the other pillow. It was the floor for him again. He was getting too old for this shit.

He was almost asleep, when she sat up in the bed.

"Mark!" He jumped up, and was next to the bed before he knew it.

"What's wrong?" he asked as he flipped on the lamp.

Megan blinked several times. What's wrong, is I'm blind. That's what." Mark had to laugh.

Megan laughed too. It was the first light moment they had had.

"I'm sorry, I woke up and it was dark and I didn't know where I was."

"Understandable".

"I'm sorry if I woke you up."

"It's ok. I wasn't asleep yet."

"You shaved." She said

"Yes...."

"You look nice."

"Thanks." he said, looking at her nervously. He was shirtless, wearing only a pair of grey sweats.

"I didn't know you had tattoos."

"I have a few." He had a tribal band around each Bicep, and a large sun on his chest, over his heart.

He had always worn long sleeve shirts, a suit Jacket, and had never been shirtless around her before. She was sitting up on her knees now, literally scoping him over.

He felt uncomfortable to say the least. He felt like an idiot. His face was turning red.

"You are blushing." She stated.

"No."

"Yes you are. You are beet red." He could feel his ears burning. "I'm warm It's hot in here."

"It's hot in here all right," she said jokingly pointing to his chest.

"Ok enough," he said, shaking his head. He grabbed his shirt off the dresser and slipped it on. She smiled, and lay back down.

He flipped the lamp off and eased back down to the floor.

He propped himself up on one arm, facing the bed. He could still feel his face glowing. He had to smile.

It was a little amusing, that she had gotten the best of him.

"Mark."

"yes?"

"Do you ever get lonely?"

"What do you mean?"

" I mean, You are alone."

"No, I don't get lonely."

"Do you have a girlfriend?"

"What?" he was flustered now.

He wasn't sure how this conversation was going or why.

"No." He replied nervously.

"Why not?" Megan asked. She rolled over and looked at him over the side of the bed.

"I don't have time." He lied.

"Have you ever had a girlfriend?"

"Of course I have. I've had a few."

"And… what happened to them?"

"Nothing, we just didn't work out."

"Why not?" She was genuinely interested now.

His palms were beginning to sweat. Now he was getting warm.

"I don't know Megan, Me , them, life…you know?"

"So…was there anyone serious?"

"No, not really…." That was the truth. He never committed to anyone. He had a few girlfriends here and there…over his lifetime, but he didn't fit with them or the lives they led.

He was gone a lot, crawling around in the mud in another world somewhere.

"I just had my work, and my job doesn't really allow for family and commitment.

That's what most Women want. I wasn't able to give that."

"And you? Don't you want that?"

What the hell… he thought. Something in him told him to be careful how he answered. This Conversation was going south fast.

"Right now I just want to keep you safe."   She sighed.

"And after?"

His heart started pounding now. It was so loud he was afraid she would hear it. He rolled onto his back.

"What do you mean?"

Right after he said it he hit himself in his forehead. He needed to shut this conversation down.

"You know."

"I don't."..... He did.

"Yes you do. I see how you look at me ."

There it was. Boom.

He rubbed his face, and his eyes, Ran his hand through his hair. He was thankful it was dark.

"I'm a professional." God what a stupid thing to say, he thought.

"Ok, but you do like me."

"Of course I like you. I'm here to protect you."

"I know you do."

"Your Father.." She suddenly interrupted him.

"MY FATHER IS DEAD."

"I know." He said quietly feeling like an ass.

"Forget it. I'm going to sleep." He heard her roll over.

He was in a frenzy. What the hell had just happened? It must have been shock and grief on her part.

After a half hour he finally relaxed. Mark was tired. He was drifting, almost asleep.

"Do you have any other family? I know you told me about your mom but there has to be someone."

Oh my god here we go again, he thought.

"No," he replied.

"None?"

"No, my mother died when I was sixteen, and I never knew my father. I was an only child, so no siblings." Few people knew these things.

"Oh, I am sorry."

He loved the sound of her voice...he caught himself thinking about how she bit her bottom lip when she spoke.

He jumped up and went to the bathroom. Mark turned on the light, starring at himself in the mirror.

They hadn't been on the road twenty four hours. He had to seriously get himself together. No more mistakes.

No more of this nonsense. He stayed in the bathroom till she was asleep. Once again there would be little sleep for him.

Nathan and Paul waited outside of the property. There was no sign of Megan or the bodyguard.

They had waited all night. Nathan sat in the back of the Van, with his head bowed. He hadn't moved in hours.

It made Paul uncomfortable to hear him chanting to whatever god he answered to.

At first light Paul walked up to the guard station.

"Can I help you sir"? The guard asked.

"I'm here to see Megan Goldberg."

"She's not here."

"Do you know when she will be back? We had an appointment." The guard turned his back to ring the house.

His eyes opened wide as the blade slid between his ribcage.

Nathan killed the guards one by one. For him it was natural.

Paul opened the front door.

It was easy to get into the house after the remaining guards fled.

Fred came walking out of the hallway. He was confused, he had expected Megan.

The albino rushed him, like a bad dream. He died slowly, for his lack of information.

Nathan moved through the house like a shadow.

There was no sound as he climbed the steps to Megan's room.

He laid down on the bed and took in the scent of the sheets.

He held the pillow to his face inhaling the sweet smell.

This was forbidden.

He knew it. So were the panties he had stolen out of the hamper.

When he had his fill of her scent, he left the house and headed back out to the van, where Paul waited.

He climbed in the back covered with the old man's blood.

He sat down and bowed his head once more.

They left the motel and had breakfast on the road.

Mark hadn't said much this morning.

He had promised himself that he was back on track, business as usual.

They had wasted too much time already.

He was ready to get to the cabin and put together the next plan.

Once they entered Wyoming he pulled into a pain and body shop.

He went inside and came back a few minutes later.

"I need eight hundred dollars. "

"For what?" she asked as she dug in her bag.

"I'm having the truck painted, and we need snow chains.

There is a diner across the street. We can eat and wait there. Three hours later the jeep was white. Mark drove six more hours.

It had started to snow late in the evening. Visibility was not good. They spoke few words, each lost in their own thoughts.

He pulled off the highway.

They had picked up some burgers and Fries, Megan was already in the bag eating.

It surprised him how much food she could put away for such a small person.

She was always eating, or wanting to eat.

Mark pulled into the parking lot, and pointed out that the name of the motel was "The Rainbow Motel." He found some humor in it. Megan didn't.

Once inside they finished eating. Megan showered, and when she came out, her long wet hair hung loosely down her back. She smelled of soap and jasmine.

Immediately he had to get himself in check. He showered, and made sure to put on a t-shirt. When he came out she was propped up, waiting.

"You've really planned this out haven't you?" She said.

"Your dad and I made most of these plans together.

I just had to do some improvising."

He was trying to give Jack the credit. She found it sweet.

He started to make his pallet on the floor. Megan insisted he sleep on the bed. He argued, but then again, he was tired and stiff.

Mark turned off the lights, except for the bathroom light that Megan had insisted he keep on.

They said goodnight. He pulled off his t-shirt, and covered up with the sheet. Mark was tired.

He heard her breathing change and knew she was asleep.

She was lying on her side, facing him.

The blanket had slipped off her shoulders. He pulled it up around her again.

Mark softly caressed her cheek.....

He pulled his hand back slowly, sighing deeply. He did like her, she was right. More than he should.

In a small way he felt like he was betraying Jack.

He was older. He didn't want to take advantage of her, or make her feel uncomfortable. The truth was he was crazy about her, but he knew enough to realize that this wasn't the right time or place.

Maybe some day when this was all over and they got back to their lives...until then, He had a job to do.

Unable to sleep, he tossed and turned for over an hour.

He finally got up, got dressed and went outside locking the door behind himself.

Mark walked out into the parking lot. It had gotten cold.

He could see his breath. The snow crinkled beneath his shoes. It was really coming down now. He knew the seasons here well.

He had spent a lot of time at the cabin

He knew when the weather came it came hard and fast, from the looks of it Mother Nature would have little mercy this winter.

Mark walked over to the jeep. He looked around.

It was late, there was no one on sight.

He pulled the screw driver out of his Jacket pocket and removed the Florida Plate.

He reached under the backseat and pulled out the Wyoming plate.

Once it was secured he bent the old one in half and tossed it into the dumpster.

He watched a tractor trailer pull into the parking lot.

Ten minutes later the driver walked by him. "Cold night huh?"

"Yeah, where you heading?"

"South, Port of Miami."

The man grumbled, as he fumbled with his keys.

"Great," mark whispered under his breath.

He watched the man walk over to the diner. He walked around to the back of the rig.

He put the battery in Megan's cell phone and wedged it into the small groove of the rear door.

The sun woke mark. It was shining on his face.

He reached up to cover his eyes. When he had finally went to sleep. He had gone out like a light.

"Wake up sleeping beauty." Megan said cheerfully.

She had opened the drapes to let the sun shine in. Mark jumped up and ripped the curtains shut.

"These can't be open." He said in a stern voice.

"I'm sorry ...I forgot." She said quietly, the smile on her face gone.

"No, I'm sorry," Mark said I shouldn't have yelled at you like that. I freaked out because I overslept."

"Well you haven't slept much in the last few days. You must have needed it." She starred at his chest and arms.

"Well let me get dressed, and then we'll get on the road.

Don't open the curtains or the door."

"If someone knocks you want me to come and get you?" she said with a sly smile on her face.

He felt his face blushing again.

"You know what I mean."

He grumbled as he stalked off toward the bathroom.

After a hot shower, he was in a better mood.

He was pissed at himself for sleeping in, but maybe he did need it, like she said.

They left the Motel and ate at the diner again since Megan refused to eat in the car. It had started to snow again.

"We need to get going. I want to be at the cabin tonight."

"It's cold here, that's for sure." She said.

"You haven't seen the half of it." He pulled out onto the highway and headed west.

"I've never seen snow before." Megan said.

"That's right you're a Florida girl." Mark said lightly.

"You will get used to it eventually. I love the mountains. I haven't been up there in years, though. I have a family that keeps it maintained for me, and even better than, that it will be hard to track because it's not in my name." She didn't answer, but continued to stare out the window at the snow.

Megan didn't talk much all that afternoon.

"What's wrong?" mark asked.

"I miss my father."

"I know I miss him too."

"But, you stay calm all the time. I never see you cry about him. I'm always the one. How do you keep so calm?"

"It's my job Megan, I try not to get involved."

Right after the words came out he wished he hadn't said them.

"Is that what I am to you, a job?"

"No of course not that's not the way I meant it."

They continued to ride in silence. The mountains rose in the distance, as the snow continued to fall.

THE CABIN

Megan slept for hours. When she woke up they only made small talk.

He stopped for gas and coffee. The weather didn't permit any long stops. Towards evening they entered the Grand Teton Pass.

Mark pulled into Grants. It was a giant supply store. They sold everything from guns to boats, to bear traps.

He had shopped there several years ago. Mark purchased a trailer and winter supplies.

Megan got boots and a winter jacket, and several warm sweaters.

They checked out separately and paid with cash. He loaded everything and rushed her into the truck. He put on the snow chains. The pass would be a bitch.

The snow was coming down hard now. Mark glanced over at Megan. He knew that look…. The look of panic. He had seen it many times before.

He knew the elevation was a contributing factor. Megan's heart pounded. She felt as if she couldn't take a deep breath. Her father was dead. She couldn't breathe….

She was alone, in the world. The trip had been exhausting.

Megan had never been away from home, and everything was unfamiliar. There was a crazed cult chasing her.

It was all too much. Mark drove on.

He kept looking at her. He could see she was in distress, but the weather was so bad, if he didn't keep driving, they would never make it through the pass.

He held her hand for a bit.

"Megan, stay with me, It's going to be ok."

She continued to cry silently. It broke his heart.

"I promise you, you will be ok. I have to keep driving, or we will never get through this weather. I don't want you to think that I don't care." There, he had said it.

Megan squeezed his hand. "Ok…"

The windy dark road stretched sixty miles across the steep mountains. It was snowing hard and he could feel the ice beneath the tires.

He was glad he had put on the snow chains.

"How much further?" Megan asked.

"Twenty miles, it's up near the top of the pass." He was shouting now, the wind had picked up and was howling. Megan tried to look out the window and caught a glimpse of the road and the steep drop off.

Her stomach turned.

"There is no guard rail." She swallowed hard.

"No. don't look down."

"You're kidding me right?"

Mark starred at the road.

Forty minutes later, he steered into a hidden driveway. Two miles down the drive, the cabin came into sight.

He prayed that old Mr. Johnson had remembered everything he had asked for.

The lights were on, that was a good sign. Mark pulled his weapon.

"Wait here." He went inside, moving quietly like a Shadow. Once the cabin and its surroundings were secure, he hurried Megan inside, and made a fire.

He had spotted the other trailer of supplies that had been delivered several weeks ago. So far, so good.

The cabin had been there for over a Hundred years. It was built well and had seen its share of storms.

Ten years ago, Mark had come up and completely remodeled the cabin.

He had installed indoor plumbing, and knew Megan would appreciate that.

He showed Megan to her bedroom. It was small but quaint.

It has a full size bed, made up with fresh sheets and a few thick quilts. Megan lay down on the bed. He pulled off her boots and covered her.

"Just lay here and relax. I'm going to unload the Jeep and get this place warm."

He would take the first room it was smaller, and closer to the door.

"How long are we going to have to stay here?" she said miserably.

"I don't know."

" We'll talk about it tomorrow. Get some rest."

He couldn't do this right now. There was too much to do.

The cabin heated up quickly. It was well insulated. It was made all of cedar, and smelled of it.

A quilt rack sat in the corner- the Amish furniture suited it well. Everything was made of wood, except the chandelier, made of deer antlers.

A large stone fireplace, that was at the other end, across from the couch that was covered with quilts.

Mark unloaded the Jeep.

He secured all the doors, and brewed himself some coffee, and stood in front of the fire rubbing his hands to warm them.

Sleep wasn't coming anytime soon. He missed the old man.

It was hard to believe that jack was dead. He had always been such a larger than life presence. Mark swallowed hard. There was that damn lump again.

He rubbed his eyes. They would be safe here for a while.

The next few days passed quickly. Mark put away all the supplies, from both trailers.

In the afternoons they gathered more wood, for the fire.

Megan moved through the motions. He let her be, and hoped she would come out of it.

She spoke few words, but would follow Mark and help with the chores. She ate very little and slept a lot.

Every day they gathered fire wood.

Mark told her it needed time to dry out so they had to keep a constant supply.

It was tedious monotonous work, but it kept them both busy.

In the evenings they drank coffee or tea and ate soup, and sandwiches.

When the weather cleared they made one last trip to the store. This would be the last.

They couldn't take any chances.

Not to mention, his last year up at the cabin the weather had been so bad, it had snowed so much he was stuck for months.

Megan watched the sun set over the mountains.

The snow flurried around. She was in awe.

It was so beautiful. It put the ocean to shame.

She wished they could have been here under different circumstances, but like Mark had said, he had a Job to do.

She had to respect that.

Slowly she came around. Maybe it was the beauty of the sun setting over the mountains, or the lazy snowflakes falling.

Whatever it was, she started to feel safe.

THE ALBINO

Anita walked quickly up the staircase.

She flung open the Albino's door.

"What have you done?"

He sat at the end of his bed naked, blood covering his hands and mouth.

The coppery smell was heavy in the air.

He dropped onto his knees.

"Priestess, forgive me. I have needs. You have forgotten me."

"Needs?" You don't get to have that liberty anymore. This is the third time this month. Where is she?"

"In the bathroom." He whispered.

She walked over and pushed the door open with her foot.

The Girls body had been flung into the tub, in a rage. Her body twisted, and mangled, her legs bent up under her, in a grotesque way.

Her nipples were savagely bitten off. With every girl, his rage became greater.

Each murder, more brutal.

He was out of control, but he was right, she had neglected him, as of late.

She had become so consumed with finding Megan that she had forgotten him.

Once, when she had first found him, he had reminded her of her childhood friend Spencer.

They grew up together in the same orphanage.

When they became teenagers they were adopted together, into the cult. They both thrived on the same beliefs, sharing their love for the dark arts.

Anita had spotted Jack, and the cult decided he had promise, and money.

The original plan had been to convince Jack, to join the cult.

Once she married him, Spencer became jealous, and she left him behind.

He later was arrested for theft, and hung himself in his cell. Anita had forgotten him as well.

A month later she found the Albino on the street.

He prowled and lured girls, telling them he was a priest. There was Sylvia from Connecticut, she had been the first.

She was a prostitute trying to find god. He gave her food and wine. Lots of wine.

The Albino carried her up the stairs and rubbed the spot between her legs, till she begged him to fuck her.

He had spread her legs wide, she screamed when he entered her. He was a freak of nature.

He felt her skin tearing.

She screamed louder, and he punched her in the face.

The site of the blood had excited him more.

He reached down and had broken her neck.

He bit off her nipples. The beast liked to save them. He had thrown her into the tub, and walked away.

Anita motioned him to her. She turned and bent over the bed.

He knew just what to do.

DRIFTING

Mark was bent intently over his laptop.

She watched him.

He was ruggedly handsome, especially now that his hair had grown out some, he needed another shave.

 She smiled thinking back to the conversation they had at the motel.

She had embarrassed him on purpose.

It was so funny, it made her smile even now.

 He thought she had been asleep when he touched her face. It was surprisingly gentle.

Mark was a large muscular man there was nothing gentle about that.

An unfamiliar feeling was coming over her, as she watched him. Her eyes traveled to his shoulders.

She like the broadness of them, and the way he towered over her when they stood next to each other.

He was nice to look at.

Her feelings were scaring her.

She knew he loved his work, and when this was all over he would move on.

He had said it himself, he never got attached.

The days moved on.

They were outside gathering their daily supply of wood.

Megan was ahead of mark.

She started to drop one of the pieces, when she grabbed it a large splinter went straight through her glove into the palm of her hand.

They dropped all the wood in the small mud room. He helped her take off her Glove, and her jacket.

He led her over to the sink. He could see the splinter it was large.

He grabbed it between his fingers.

Megan snatched her hand away.

"What are you going to do? It hurts."

"I was going to pull it out." He said.

"Well, be careful." She commanded.

He smiled. He pulled the splinter out and ran her hand under the warm water.

When they both looked up they were face to face.

Their eyes locked.

His heart fluttered.

He moved away suddenly.

"I have to get the first aid kit."

She studied him closely.

He was nervous.

He came back with Neosporin and a band aid.

His big hands were trembling. He fumbled with the tape.

"Are you ok?" she asked.

"Yes, I am." He answered quickly.

"Your hands are shaking."

"Well I had too much coffee."

The last few days it had taken all of Marks might to push the front door open.

It was going to be a long winter. The snow fell by the foot.

Soon they would be snowed in.

THE PAST

The days passed slowly.

They tried to get out for a walk at least once a day.

It broke up the day and gave them both a chance to get fresh air.

It gave Mark a chance to look for any tracks that shouldn't be there.

In the last few days there were Coyotes and bears, nothing more.

They talked for hours on end.

He told her of his life with the Agency.

It was something he had never discussed before.

Dark things about himself he had never told a living soul.

He talked of missions and the things he didn't agree with, and how once he had voiced them they had left him in a Sudi prison camp to rot with his men.

Luckily a friend at the state department had him released.

His men were dead. He was the only one left.

He made his way to Malaysia and holed up in a hut for weeks staying drunk.

Then he went back to the states, got himself together, and returned to the camp to make things right, for his Men.

He was in and out like a ghost. A shadow Man.

They never saw him coming.

Once again he flew home and started working security.

"How did my dad find you"? Megan asked.

"Your father was very well connected.

He knew important people.

He knew some of my past.

I didn't think he would hire me knowing I was a sniper, but he said he needed someone that wouldn't be afraid to kill if it was needed.

I thought he was just being overprotective.

I wasn't even going to take the job. It was too domestic for me.

Especially when I found out it would be you I was guarding."

"Well thanks a lot." Megan joked.

It's not even like that.

I was used to guarding men. Politicians, businessmen.

Not a teenager.

The first few years I was bored out of my skull, but somehow I stayed on. Your father was easy to like. I miss him a lot." He concentrated on the falling snow, to keep his emotions in check.

"Then you both became like a family to me." Megan saw his lip trembling. She looked away, not wanting to embarrass him. He had feelings after all.

"It became harder and harder to leave and the years just kept going by." He said. Pushing snow around with his foot.

"Then I couldn't leave, a few months after that was when the cult thing started. You know the rest."

They entered the cabin, and pulled off their boots and jackets. He felt like a heel.

Things had been going so good, and he still hadn't told her about Jack being murdered.

Mark put on a pot of coffee.

"My father really liked you. He had a lot of respect for you and he loved you like a son."

They sat on the small couch in the main room.

"It means a lot, to hear you say that."

THE CULT

I've been researching the cult. They have so many connections.

Recently though, a few members have started dropping out, and they came up missing.

If we can find one person and get them to talk it may be just what we need.

Then there was an incident at a ranch in Texas, two cult members went to the papers, both of them and the reporter were killed.

This is not small time anymore, but they are making mistakes, and powerful people don't like publicity.

It may be heading in the direction we need it to.

The cult worships one high priestess.

She had to have a direct descendant from her bloodline in order to ascend.

It's some kind of ritual that has to happen for her to gain full power.

She needs you, or the cult can't go on.

There is much more to it.

I was able to get into the classified access.

I found out that the direct descendant has to be pure.

"What does that mean?"

"It means if you are a virgin it will bring the ultimate power."

Megan could feel her face turning bright red.

He watched her face, carefully. Wondering what she was thinking.

"A virgin will strengthen the circle, and this ritual had to take place on one of the Solstices. They prefer the one on the cusp of the yearning. Whatever that means.

I'm still trying to find out, but my point is that they follow the left hand path.

They are Satanists, and they are into some creepy shit."

"Do you think that's why they want me so badly?"

"What do you mean."?

"The virgin Part."

He starred at her, narrowing his eyes.

He had not thought this out to the end.

"Megan, tell me you are not a virgin. You are 23 years old for gods sake."

He starred at her.

She starred back, and shrugged her shoulders.

His mind reeled. She was right.

There had been no one. He had always been there, on every date.

He had just assumed that before him, or sometime or another.

Well, he never really thought about it.

Now more than ever he knew she was the one thing they needed more than anything, and they were willing to kill for it.

"Maybe if I loose my virginity they won't want me."

She said desperately.

"I don't know...I mean who could we get...?"

She was staring at him now.

"What do you mean, who could we get?"

"Well,"... she said, as the realization dawned on him.

"No....OH NO....not me, I can't do that."

"Why not?"

"Because, I don't do that sort of thing." He was completely flustered.

That's not what I was hired for. God, I sound so stupid, Megan, I'm sorry.

It just never occurred to me."

He was pacing now.

"You have to help me." She pleaded.

Mark sighed hard and closed his eyes.

He was standing still with his hands on his head.

He was embarrassed, his face flushed.

He was a grown man.

It was ridiculous.

He should not be embarrassed he had lots of experience.

He knew what he was doing.

"Megan….."

"Please Mark…I've never asked you for anything. I mean my god how bad can it be?"

He suddenly had the overwhelming urge to laugh.

She thought that he didn't want to, because he wouldn't like it. The furthest thing from the truth. He had wanted her for weeks.

Now he had the opportunity to be a hero even, and he was scared out of his mind. He sighed.

"Ok, I'll do it, but I say when. I'm not a trained Monkey you know."

"I'm taking a walk." he said storming off.

He slid on his boots and Jacket, and headed outside.

The sun was out for once and there were only Flurries.

He checked out the barn and the area around the cabin.

When he deemed it was safe he walked down the long drive toward the road.

The fresh air felt good to him. Mark started to jog. The snow crunched under his feet.

It felt good. He was used to running 6 miles a day.

He had to think about this whole situation.

She thought he didn't want to sleep with her.

He was ashamed to say that it had been crossing his mind an awful lot.

He loved the way she smelled, and the way she looked.

Hell, he loved everything about her. It wasn't just a job anymore.

Mark had cared for Jack, and her, but since the trip it had turned into something more.

There was no fighting it anymore.

He wanted her but he wasn't sure if it was the right thing.

He still fought with his promise to Jack, and his Job he had sworn to do.

He came in from his walk.

She had made dinner and was eating.

"Hey"

"Hi".

He made himself a plate and sat down beside her at the small wooden table.

"What's going to happen when this is over Mark?"

"What do you mean?"

He could tell there was an edge to her voice.

"We go home, and carry on with our lives."

"But what are YOU going to do.

Your Job will be done.

You said so yourself, this is a job to you and you never get attached."

If there was ever a moment when he wished there was something he didn't say, this was it.

"Are you trying to get rid of me?"

He said trying to lighten the mood. "No it's your Job."

She was starting to piss him off.

"So as soon as this is over you're on to the next Client? Am I right?" she continued to eat.

"No, I mean, I don't know."

What are you getting at?"

"I know what you're going to say…" she said smugly.

You're the only one who can protect me."

"That's right." Mark answered angrily.

"Well Mr. Hot Shot, aren't you full of yourself."

She stood up in front of him with her hands on her hips.

He was really getting out of sorts now. He dropped his fork in his plate.

"The truth is the truth."

"So you keep telling me." He stood up and threw his plate into the sink, food and all.

Now he was yelling. "Damn Megan what is your problem? All I was trying to say was that I know how to protect you, and you don't want to let me do it properly.

This is no Joke. These people are no Joke. They are killers.

They will kill me, you, any one that gets in their way."

"I guess as a trained killer, you would know this."

She shot back.

Mark closed his eyes, and attempted to regain his composure.

He tried to control his breathing.

He was very close to losing his cool.

Mark paced back and forth, telling himself to walk it off.

"I'll bet you never gave a shit about my father either. He was just a job too."

Mark turned and punched the door frame.

It was the only release he had.

Megan turned and ran to her room, slamming her door.

He punched the frame again.

His hand ached, the doorframe was cracked. "Fuck" he said under his breath.

He walked outside and stuck his hand in the snow.

When he came back in Megan was standing in the kitchen.

"Mark, I am so sorry. I had no right to say those things to you, and I understand that this is your job but in the last few weeks...."

He interrupted her.

"It's ok." He stated.

"I understand. You are stressed, and out of your element.

Your away from home, you just lost your dad. I get it."

"That's not it I..." He interrupted again.

"You don't have to keep apologizing."

"Damn, Mark I'm not trying to apologize.

What I'm trying to say is that in the last few weeks, I've really gotten to know you and, I've fallen in love with you."

He stood there and stared.

He was trying to process her words.

"It's ok, you don't have to say anything. I know you take this very serious, and I know you don't feel the same. I will let you do your job." A tear ran down her cheek.

His heart pounded in his chest.

This was it.

The moment he had to decide which way this was going to go.

He reached over and gently touched her face stroking her hair.

"I don't want to hurt you."

"Then don't." she whispered.

"You have become my whole life." He said.

"You are everything to me."

He leaned in and took her face in both hands and kissed her. Mark pulled her into his arms and her and kissed her again.

"I love you."

He had never said this to a single person. Not ever.

His relationships had been trivial at best. There were few.

His work had taken him all over the world.

He had seen lots of people and places, but this was entirely new for him.

She scared the shit out of him. He held her for a long time. They didn't speak.

Much later they cleaned up from dinner, and swept up the splinters from the doorframe.

He showered, and came out to make them a pallet on the floor in front of the fire.

It was an extremely cold night. He put more logs on the fire.

Megan came out of the bathroom.

She stood in front of him and dropped her robe.

He starred at her naked body as if he had never seen one before.

It was almost too much to bear.

His self- control was slipping away from him quickly.

"Megan, god I want you so badly, but I just don't know if it will be safe." He rubbed his chin in thought

"It may be our only hope...your virginity....." He pulled the robe up and draped it gently around her.

"There will be a time for us, not like this."

He had no more doubts about the way he felt for her.

He just didn't want this to cost her, her life.

She tilted her head to the side and sighed.

Her long hair hung loosely around her shoulders. She caressed his face. "Ok."

They lay down on the makeshift bed he had built.

The fire was going well, and lit up the room with a sensual light.

She lay down next to him in her robe.

He knew there was nothing on underneath. It made him crazy.

He held her and kissed her until she fell asleep.

The cabin had grown dark. Mark got up and put another log on the fire.

He checked the windows and doors. He was upset with himself.

 He wasn't sure if it was because he did the one thing that Grey had always taught him not to do.

Get involved, fall in love, or the fact that he picked up that damn robe.

Whichever it was it didn't matter now. All that mattered was that he loved her, and she loved him.

It was more than he had ever expected.

Paul ran out to meet Anita's car. By the look on his face she knew it was bad.

"What's wrong?"

"He's gone crazy."

"What the hell are you talking about?

"Nathan"

"What do you mean."

She followed him to the bunk house.

He killed them all. The bunk house housed 12 men.

They were her inner circle. She had hand- picked all of them.

She entered the bunk house. The overwhelming small of blood filled her nostrils.

The bodies were scattered. Three of the men's throats were slashed.

A few had broken necks.

Others were mangled beyond belief.

It looked like a wild animal had come through. In a strange way, it had.

"Where is he now?" she asked.

"In the house."

"What set him off?"

"The guys caught him with that picture of Megan, he stole from the house. He stole her panties too. The guys were making fun of him. He just went crazy."

"Alright. I'm going to go and see about him. I'll call the cleaners. They will get rid of all this. Go wait for them by the gate."

"Are you sure we shouldn't call the police?"

"We can't call them. Go wait by the gate."

Normally she would have gone off on him, but right now she had bigger fish to fry.

Anita entered the house. "NATHAN."

"Where are you?" her sickingly sweet voice resonated through the house.

She walked up the steps and opened his door.

He sat on the bed. She smelled soap on him.

He had showered and wore a fresh robe.

"You have been a very bad boy, Nathan."

"They were mocking the most high priestess."

"She isn't your priestess. I am."

"Yes".

"Say it"

"You are the priestess."

Anita heard the men come up the stairs.

"Just checking on you priestess. Are you ok?"

"Yes."

She turned to the Albino, "Nathan, you will go with these men to the basement. You must go to the cage. You know the punishment for disobeying. Do you understand?"

"Yes."

He unfolded his hands and looked up at the men with his eerie pink eyes.

"Take him."

THE MOUNTAIN

Mark woke up early. He tapped the glass on the widow.

Enough snow fell off to see that it was almost white out conditions.

He flipped on the weather radio, while he made coffee.

The announcer said conditions were favorable for a blizzard, and could range from a week, to ten days.

Mark knew they had plenty of supplies.

A blizzard for them meant safety.

No one would be venturing up the mountain in the next few days.

He grabbed his cup and sat down at the table.

He turned on the laptop to see if there was any word from Grey.

Grey had trained him in the Special forces.

He had taught him everything.

They had become friends, and kept in touch, although he hadn't seen him in 6 Years.

Megan came into the kitchen.

He pulled her into his arms and kissed her.

"Morning beautiful."

"Morning. Is there coffee?"

He poured her a cup.

She took it with her to the bathroom.

Mark studied the computer. There was a reference to the spring equinox, and the Summer Solstice, on the classified search engine that Grey had hooked him up with.

Grey had sent an attached e-mail saying that he thought the Summer solstice was definitely the date that they meant to use.

It was the longest day of the year and the cult considered it to be the most important day in the earth's cycle. June 21st.

There was also the mid summers eve on June 23rd but Grey didn't think it was important.

He trusted his judgement.

He had less than six months to figure out what to do, as far as the ritual was concerned.

Megan came back into the room, and sat next to him at the table. She was dressed in jeans and a soft pink sweater.

Mark briefly explained what he had found, and Who Grey was, and how they had met.

They talked as they made and ate breakfast.

There would be no walk today, not with the weather bearing down on them.

They sat down on the couch, together.

"About last night," Mark said.

"I meant every word I said to you, but when emotions are involved it's easy to make a mistake.

Any small mistake can cost us everything."

"I trust you," she said. He leaned in and kissed her.

He wanted her so badly. He caressed her face and hair, and she ran her hands under his shirt, over his shoulders and back. She pulled his shirt over his head, and they continued to kiss. He felt his self- control slipping away.

"Megan, you are killing me." He sat back and sighed deeply.

"I love you, and I want you so much, but we have to wait."

Mark pulled his shirt back on.

He reached over and pulled the Maps off the small end table.

"We need to route out a couple different ways to get out of here, in case they find us before the weather breaks.

I need you to know the routes too and to be able to read this map in case something happens to me.

He showed her the routes he had highlighted.

There was a Ranger station that would provide shelter, and there was the cave, and he had mapped out the route to Grey's Fortress.

Another way through the Snake River canyon, and lastly the way straight up.

50 miles of ice and snow, with no shelter, a last resort.

"There is something I need to tell you."

He sighed, and took her hand and held it.

"There are two things. First, Your Father was murdered."

He looked at her, Waiting for a response.

He hoped she wouldn't hate him for waiting so long.

"I know." She said.

"You knew?" Mark starred at her in disbelief.

"Yes. When I found him, I looked him over.

He had puncture marks in his neck, and he had an amulet around his neck that I know wasn't his."

"I didn't tell the police. Something just told me not to. So I hid it in my pocket."

"All this time you have been carrying this."

"Why didn't you tell me?"

"I didn't want you to leave me, to go after some killer. It's selfish I know. But I didn't know what else to do."

"It's ok. I wouldn't have left you."

The computer binged.

Mark got up to check the e-mail from Grey.

"What does it say?" Megan asked.

"It says….The cult has a tradition to pass a descendant down the bloodline. That's you. If they don't perform the ritual by the deadline of the spring equinox,

Consisting of you taking Anita's place so she can move up to the highest spot, then the only way for her to ascend is a sacrifice."

"She has to sacrifice her bloodline to keep her power."

Mark sighed.

Megan was staring at him.

"You mean if I don't join them by the Equinox, they will kill me."

"I am the sacrifice...right?"

"It looks that way." He replied. "I'm sorry."

"This is surreal. It's stuff out of some nightmare. This shit doesn't happen. I guess it's not enough, that my father's been murdered, my mother's a psycho cult bitch, and I'm in hiding."

Tears ran down her cheeks.

She put her hands over her face as she cried.

Mark put his arms around her. He held her. She sat up finally.

"What else do you have to tell me?"

"I wanted to tell you that if something were to happen to me, you need to go to Grey's. He will protect you. You need to be prepared if the worst happens."

He stood up. Megan liked how he looked in his blue jeans and a white T- shirt. It was much nicer than the suits.

"Come on I want to show you something."

Megan followed him to the attic. "There are more food rations up here, and ammo for the guns. There's also a tent."

"What's that?" she pointed to an old dog sled.

"That, is Grey's dog sled. He ran the Ididterod for a few years across Alaska. I was his storage for a while."

They climbed back down the ladder.

"Put on your Jacket I have something else to show you."

"In the blizzard?"

"It's not a blizzard yet." He smiled.

He had already slipped on his jacket, and was walking out the door.

The fresh air felt good. He breathed deep. He loved the cold.

The snow had let up a little. Megan chased after Mark.

"Wait for me," she yelled as she hopped along trying to get her second boot on.

Mark headed around the side of the cabin.

There was a small trail barely discernable in the snow.

They walked for about ten minutes.

Megan brushed limbs away from her face and rushed to keep up with his fast pace.

Soon they came to a solid mountain wall.

Mark walked along the wall and seemed to be looking for something.

Suddenly he disappeared into a small opening in the rock.

Megan followed.

It was narrow for a moment, then slowly widened into a large cave with a pool of steaming water in the middle. The temperature was at least 30 degrees warmer.

"Well, what do you think?" he asked.

"It's beautiful. How did you find it?

"On a hunting trip, the place has probably been here for a thousand years."

He kicked off his boots and stripped off his jacket and shirt.

"Come on are you getting in or what?"

Megan stood there dumb founded as he dropped his pants.

She stared at his naked body, as he walked into the water.

He was tan and muscular. His shoulder's massive.

He walked out a few feet, then began to swim.

Once she got down to her bra and panties she stood there, nervously. Mark noticed.

"Leave those on and come on." He said rushing her to alleviate her fear.

She sighed with relief and walked out into the water. It was hot.

"This feels great."

"Yeah it's great for the old stiff bones."

I wouldn't know about that." She teased.

Mark smiled. He was glad her mood had lightened.

They swam and talked for a while, and eventually lay in the shallow water on their belly's talking.

Mark's naked back and bottom protruded from the water.

She was looking him over.

Once she looked up their eyes met. Megan felt her face flushing. Their gaze held for a long while.

Finally Mark broke the gaze and looked away.

He loved her there was no doubt. He wanted to make love to her right here in the Water, but he had a plan. He had thought about it all night.

Since the virgin part was not important anymore as far as her safety was concerned, all bets were off.

He was waiting for tonight.

Everything needed to be perfectly dark so the fire would be the only light in the room. He could hardly wait.

Mark rolled over on his side.

He caressed her cheek. She pulled his hand to her lips and kissed it. He caressed her back, her breast, he kissed her neck. It had to wait till tonight.....

"Megan we have to stop."

"No.....I don't want to stop." She continued to kiss him.

He touched her body, running his hands over her belly and under her bra. She moaned as he manipulated her nipples gently, Rubbing them between his fingers. He pulled her bra up and ran his tongue over each one.....slowly. He caressed her thigh, and moved down, sliding his hand inside her panties. She was wet.

 He slowly worked his way to that special spot, rubbing in a circular motion. First slowly then faster, until her hips came up off the ground, and she moaned loudly as she came.

When she caught her breath he kissed her.

"Now, calm down and lets go." He whispered.

He kissed her again, until a flurry of leaves flew into the opening.

Mark looked up. "We better go, the wind is picking up.

The storm must be gaining strength."

 They dressed quickly, holding hands as he pulled her along behind him.

Later the snow eased up again.

They loaded two backpacks and started the Snowmobile.

He had a feeling he needed to show her the mountain while he could.

While there was time. His gut instinct was hardly ever wrong.

He took her as far as the ranger station, and pointed out Landmarks to the different locations.

She needed to have some idea of where to go if the worst happened.

The lack of conversation made Megan nervous, but she had promised to trust him.

The cabin finally came into view. She went inside and heated soup for them while he put the snowmobile away.

 The day had started so nicely, then suddenly out of nowhere, the feelings came over him, that he couldn't shake. The fear of coming dread.

"Why are you being so quiet?" Megan asked.

"I just have a feeling that as soon as the weather breaks they are going to be all over this place. I don't know where it came from. I can't shake it."

RUNNING

Anita paced back and forth outside the bunk house.

The car pulled up. Rob exited the car. He had worked intel for her in the past.

He was a hacker and she counted on him to find things others could not.

So far he had never disappointed her.

"Well?" she asked impatiently.

"The bodyguards name is Mark Westbrook. Jack hired him five years ago.

He was in the Army, and then the Special forces.

After that, nothing. After 2011, he doesn't exist.

My guess is he's a Man in black. A Cloak- and- Dagger man.

They worked for the Government. Off the grid. They go in to clean up, assassinate, kill, make things and people disappear."

"Great, now we are dealing with a fucking Ghost."

"The men from the southern Region will be here tonight." He reminded her.

"Someone better find this "Ghost", because if I don't get Megan, I can't ascend, and if I can't ascend everybody dies."

Mark made a special dinner of Spaghetti with meat sauce, and salad.

It was the last of the fresh vegetables they had picked up at the store.

After dinner they sat in front of the fire.

The wind howled outside

"What are we going to do? Where can we possibly go?"

"Up the mountain, to Grey's. We just have to stay one step ahead."

"It will be thanksgiving in a few days."

"Yes, I know."

"Remember that awful casserole my dad made every year? The one no one wanted to eat?" She smiled.

"The one with the green stuff." Mark shuddered at the thought.

"Yes, that raggedy dog he had wouldn't even eat it."

"Fred ate it."

The smile faded from Mark's face.

"What?" the smile had left her face also.

"Fred is dead."

"What? How?"

"They killed him, and the guards."

"They are going to kill me too aren't they?"

"I'm not going to let that happen."

She sat in silence for a moment.

"I'll tell you one thing. As of this moment, I'm going to live my life. I'm not wasting another moment."

Mark put his arms around her.

He held her for a while, then when the fire got low, he stood and put more wood on.

By the time Megan came back from the bathroom he had made their pallet in front of the fire.

He watched her cross the room in her robe, the same robe that she dropped for a second time.

This time he didn't pick it up. He stepped back and looked at her body. He sighed, longingly, and pulled her to him. Her skin was soft as satin.

He caressed her neck and kissed his way down her neck to her shoulders and back up. He caressed her breasts, while she ran her hands over his back and arms.

They lay down on the blankets. He continued to touch her, her nipples were hard under his touch.

She moaned softly as his hand traveled across her flat belly.

Mark inched his way up one thigh and down the other….His tongue circling her nipples, first one then the other.

His hand traveling to that sweet spot between her legs.

Mark moved his fingers in a circular motion, while her hips raised, and she moaned with pleasure. "Oh keep doing that…" she whispered.

He leaned in her ear.

"If I need any assistance, I'll ask…."

He moved down between her legs, raising her legs over his shoulders. She gasped as he sucked on her inner thigh…working his way to the center, lightly flicking his tongue from side to side, then in a circular motion, until she cried out with pleasure.

Eventually he moved on top of her and slowly entered her. She cried out as the pleasure mixed with pain….The pain soon subsided.

He made love to her slowly.

Kissing …licking…and lightly biting her neck and lip.

He sat up and pulled her into his lap, wrapping his arms around her, pulling her closer.

He held her face in his hands as he pushed into her harder and more passionately…."I love you ." he whispered.

Megan was beyond words as she came over and over.

Finally, he could old out no longer…he came with a guttural groan.

The cabin had grown dark. Mark woke suddenly. They were wrapped in each other's arms, naked.

He pulled himself free and put another log on the fire.

The room heated up quickly.

He drank a large glass of water.

Mark studied her….she was so beautiful.

Her long hair fanned out on the blanket.

Her shoulder and breast exposed, in the firelight, as she slept.

He lay down next to her and pulled her to him. He entered her more fiercely this time, as her legs went around him.

He made love to her for a long while before he let himself finish.

They curled up together, after a hot shower.

She fell asleep quickly. Mark opened his eyes.

The room was dark.

Something had roused him out of a deep sleep.

He slipped on his sweats and grabbed the 9mm. He knew the cabin well, moving effortlessly in the dark.

Peering out of the small window he saw two men looking at the Jeep. He moved back to Megan. He knelt down next to her ear.

"Megan, get up, get dressed now." He disappeared into the dark.

She woke in an instant, and quickly pulled on her clothes. She was just putting the last boot on, when he came back.

"Get your Jacket and your gear", he whispered.

"When I say so, you go out the back door. Get on the snowmobile, and head to the Ranger station. I will meet you there."

"No....what about you?" she was in a panic.

"Go...now...you don't wait for me." Her heart pounded.

He pushed her out the back door, and headed around to the front.

She had just gotten on the snowmobile when several shots rang out. "Oh my god..." she whispered.

She covered her ears, heart pounding out of her chest.

Suddenly all was quiet. She stood still waiting, in the dark, frantically, deciding what to do. Megan tried to slow her breathing.

The back door opened. "Are you ok?" Mark pulled her inside.

"Oh my God are you ok?" she threw her arms around him, as he winced with pain.

"What's happened?" Where are they?"

"You have to go." He held his side.

"They had a CB and were talking to someone. There will be more. You have the maps. Go north straight up, don't stop for anything.

When you get to the main road go left… 6 or seven miles, on the left you'll see a large column. Turn there. Grey will help you."

"What the hell are you talking about?" Megan flipped on the kitchen light, and saw the large red stain soaking his shirt.

"Oh my god you've been shot."

"It's nothing. A sniper clipped me from the woods."

He was losing ground quickly. She watched the color drain from his face.

"You need to go now…." He blinked several times.

She watched the blood drip on the floor.

"I'll head them off." He said, as he went down.

Megan's adrenaline went into overdrive.

She was thinking clearer that she ever had, no way was she leaving without him.

She had lost too much already.

She ran to get the first aid kit, and tapped a large pressure gauze over the wound.

That would have to do for now.

She covered him with one of the blankets.

She attempted to pull him out the door. He was just too heavy for her.

She ran to the attic and pulled down the ladder, dragging the sled down the stairs.

She rolled him onto the sled, and pulled it out the back door. It tied easily to the back hook of the snowmobile.

She covered him up and went around the front.

The sun was just coming up.

The carnage of bodied startled her. They were all dead.

Blood soaked the snow.

She had no idea how he had killed them all.

Once inside she grabbed Marks back pack and propped his feet with it.

She pulled her own pack on. Megan studied the map for a moment.

She started the snowmobile and headed north. She traveled for a half mile or so,

Stopping to pull a large pine branch from the tree and backtracked on foot.

She swept the tracks with the branch and walked backwards toward the Snowmobile.

North on the trail towards the Snake River canyon.

Megan stopped once to refuel the snow mobile. Mark was breathing normally, but his color was pale.

She covered his face and head to keep him warm. She entered the canyon just as it was getting dark.

Just down the slope the Ranger station came into view.

Once the snowmobile was at the doorway, it was easy to pull him off the sled into the room.

Despite the cold she was sweating. She log rolled him to the wood burner.

Luckily someone had left a few bundles of kindling.

She lit it, and felt the room begin to heat up.

Ten minutes later the packs and the sled were pulled into the ranger station, and propped against the far wall.

Megan knew she had to hurry.

The snow mobile started easy, and once around back it was covered with a white tarp.

The snow came down heavier and wet now, and the wind had picked up.

Megan's hair was frozen to her head.

The damp snow was a blessing in disguise. All the tracks that had been made were already disappearing.

She dropped her Jacket into the chair.

Mark's Jacket and Boots came off next.

Luckily he was completely dry.

A large circle of blood stained his shirt.

She rolled him over.

It looked like the bullet had gone completely through.

Water soon boiled in the pot on the small stove.

She cleaned his wound, and cauterized the hole to stop the bleeding.

She had seen her father do it once, on his thumb.

She covered the entire area.

Once again she stood and crossed the room, latching the heavy bolt, on the door.

The wind howled loudly.

It was designed for blizzard conditions. It was a one room solid wood cabin, with a wood stove and one chair.

She closed the shutters.

Suddenly she was exhausted.

Her wet pants and jacket soon hung over the chair, to dry.

Megan added a pouch of soup mix to the remaining hot water.

She sipped it slowly.

Once it was gone she stretched out beside him and went to sleep.

Several times during the night she woke up cold, putting more logs on the fire, and checked Mark for bleeding.

There was some oozing, but the wound seemed to be intact.

In the morning Megan contemplated taking him to town.

To a hospital.

He wouldn't wake up. She yelled his name.

Megan paced the room trying to decide.

His words came back to her, to trust him, and to not go towards town but rather up the Mountain to grey's.

It was over 50 miles straight up.

It would take at least a day or two.

She had the tent, but not much food.

It wouldn't be enough, especially if she got lost or had any trouble finding Grey.

The worst scenario of all, If he wasn't there.

There was only one thing to do.

She had to go back to the cabin for supplies.

She covered him and kissed his forehead, after placing the 40 caliber on the floor beside him.

Once the 9mm was tucked in her pants she scribbled a note on the back of the map and taped it to his chest with the medical tape from the first aid kit.

Outside, the cold hit her like a ton of bricks.

Her throat was sore, and her body ached.

It seemed much colder than before. Megan pulled her jacket tighter around herself.

Once the sled was hooked to the snowmobile the trip was easier.

The snow was coming down, but not as hard as the day before.

With no weight to pull she made good time.

Pulling over at the tree line she studied the cabin.

There was no movement.

She could barely make out the bodies, the snow had covered most of them.

After ten minutes, when she was convinced she was alone, Megan unhooked the sled and pulled it to the cabin.

There were still blood stains on the ground.

There was a foot, or and arm protruding from each one. She counted ten.

How he had killed them all was a mystery to her.

He was willing to die for her, that much was clear.

The sled was stocked with food, blankets, and first aid supplies. She grabbed the guns and ammo from the attic.

They could last a month, with adequate shelter.

Megan looked around one last time taking in the familiar scent of the cabin.

It had become home, in a short time.

She hoped she would live to see it again.

The sled was heavy. Megan reached the snowmobile and hooked then together.

Once again the tracks were swept clean with a pine branch.

The snow picked up again, just in time.

Mother Nature would take care of the rest of the tracks.

Four hours had passed.

The ranger station came into view.

The group of men waited anxiously in the small motel, at the Edge of the pass.

When the Snow let up she hurried to the waiting truck.

Another followed.

They rode in silence. Anita thought back to her brief life with Jack.

He had been a good husband, but she had felt no guilt when she had killed him.

Her life had no meaning until the Cult swept her up.

She had waited all these years, now she would have what she wanted.

The last transmission they had received was that the man was dead and the girl was inside.

She hoped he had suffered.

Then the weather had taken over and there was no more radio, and no way up the pass.

Anita had paced for hours, tearing at her hair and skin.

Now she sat like a stone with an odd smile on her face.

James watched her from the back seat.

He wondered how she had grown so powerful so fast.

Then again, he had followed her himself, during his darkest time.

She had found him on the verge of suicide.

His wife of 30 years had passed away suddenly of an aneurism.

He was in debt to his ears, and at the end of his rope.

She had picked him up off the ground so to speak, and payed his debts, even paying for the funeral.

She had bedded him on more than one occasion, the sex was rough and exciting.

For a while he had thought he loved her.

Then as the last year went by he had watched the same scenario with countless others.

The cult members themselves that surrounded Anita, were not rich.

They had the bare essentials, it took to live.

The money came from the higher members. The senators, and politicians, Doctors and lawyers, that used Anita and her henchmen to do their bidding.

They had made more than one wife, partner, relative, or enemy disappear.

The cult had given him peace of mind.

Then she had brought in the Albino freak.

He was glad she didn't bring him.

It wasn't long after that thigs had really gotten out of control.

James wanted no more of it.

He hoped this mountain would be his escape.

He knew how to survive in the wild.

He had hunted for years. He could live off the land.

"Almost there..." Anita said in a trance like voice.

Her smile made the hair on his Arms stand up.

The cabin came into site.

The trucks stopped and they got out

The bodied were scattered everywhere. Animal tracks and torn flesh all around.

It reminded him of a war zone, he had seen once in a previous life.

The smile faded from Anita's face.

"Check the cabin." She instructed the men.

They emerged a few moments later.

"She's not here."

"What the FUCK do you mean she's not here? Where the hell could she be? Look around she had to be here, there is nowhere to go."

Her high pitched voice became shriller and louder.

Anita rubbed her temples. No one dared to speak.

"Well it looks like this MR. Westbrook Is going to be a problem.

Get rid of the bodies. "

It took hours to bury them. The ground was frozen solid.

No one noticed James slip away.

He hid in the shed till the men left.

They traveled in several trucks, he wasn't missed.

He packed food into a bag he found in the cabin.

He hoped the girl was safe. He was done with all the killing.

Once the winter passed he would make his way to Florida and live with the boys, his sons Matt and Jeff. They were good boys.

He felt his pocket, to make sure the disc was secure. It would be his ace in the hole.

It was easy to get into her office she had trusted him.

Anita had torn his pants down and bent over the desk, begging him to fuck her.

He had done his duty.

By then he already hated her.

The bile rose in his throat thinking of it.

He glanced at the computer, and an idea was born.

Their encounter was cut short, by the men screaming.

The freak had killed another prostitute.

Anita had run out of the office.

He grabbed a blank disc off the top and downloaded her files.

It was easy the, screen was already up.

The files contained a list of every member and every dirty detail, on each one.

Anita had never asked about his past.

All she had seen was a distraught man, penniless, with no hope, but on the contrary, James had been something in his time.

For years he had been one of the most respected Government hackers the army had, ever had.

As he passed by the bodies, he Knew Mark Westbrook had to be Special Forces, black ops, or something darker.

It brought a smile to his face.

THE CAVE

Mark opened his eyes. For a moment he didn't know where he was.

He looked around and recognized the Ranger station.

Mark rolled over on his side. The pain brought his memory back quickly.

He'd gotten himself shot.

A note was taped to his shirt. After reading it he shook his head.

She was out there alone. The storm raged. He could hear the wind howl.

Mark managed to get onto his knees. One knee up he got to his feet and stumbled to the chair.

"Son of a bitch..." he whispered.

The window was in sight.

Once the shutter was pulled up he could see that the snow was really coming down.

He knew he was too weak to track her on foot.

All he could do was wait.

For the first time in his life he felt helpless.

He leaned back against the chair, and closed his eyes.

Mark must have dozed off again.

The cold blast of air woke him suddenly as the door flew open.

Megan stepped inside with her arms full of fire wood.

Everything fell to the floor, when she saw him.

"Oh my God you're ok..." she cried as she threw her arms around him.

"Whoa, easy ,don't put me back out of commission."

"I'm just glad you are all right."

"I was worried about you, out there alone.

I shouldn't have put you in that position."

He pulled her down into his lap and hugged her as tight as he could.

He kissed her and told her he loved her.

When she stood up she saw tears in his eyes.

She brought in the rest of the supplies.

Once the fire was built, they ate soup Pouches, and sardines.

Megan changed his dressings.

The wound had bled.

She scolded him for getting up.

Once his bandages were changed the room was warm.

They lay down on the blanket together, and she told him of the scene at the cabin.

The wind howled so loudly she had to repeat herself a few times.

The weather had been a blessing.

At least for tonight, they were safe.

Megan kissed him gently, and slowly unbuttoned his shirt.

She pulled off his pants and undressed in front of him.

Megan lay back down beside him and ran her hands over his body.

He quivered, with longing for her.

She moved on top of him and put him inside of her, then

moving up and down slowly…. "Jesus, I don't have to worry about the cult killing me.

You're going to beat them to it." He whispered in her ear.

"Don't worry ….I'll protect you."

The wind howled. Mark opened his eyes.

He was feeling better. His side still ached.

It took him five minutes to stand, as he gritted his teeth.

When Megan woke up she saw he had the map spread out before him.

"Are you sure you should be up?"

"yes, I'm fine."

He stood, pulling her to him. He kissed her.

"You feel warm" he said.

"I feel fine." She replied.

"We need to get moving .When the weather breaks they will be all over this mountain."

"I didn't think there were any left."

"Not even close you can bet there are more, and they will keep on coming.

We have to find somewhere to hide till I get back on my feet.

I won't risk your life again. I let my guard down.

 It won't happen again."

"You killed them all. We are safe."

"I'm just pissed off at myself for screwing up. I'm supposed to be the one protecting you, remember? And you had to take care of me."

He was proud of her.

He had no idea how she had managed to drag him all the way up here, but he was grateful.

Megan loaded the sled.

He helped as much as he could until she scolded him for it.

He handed her the map.

You drive, I'll sit on the back.

When you get to the edge of the next pass, turn left.

"I thought we were heading straight up to Grey's?

"We are, but not just yet.

There is no way we will make it in this weather.

 You see those clouds there?" He pointed to the sky.

"There is going to be a blizzard."

They loaded up and drove for twenty miles or so.

"You see that low branch there?" he pointed.

"Go left." He yelled in her ear.

It was hard to hear, the wind was coming from the north, and was blowing at them full force.

 Megan's face felt frozen.

"There is no path here." She yelled back at him.

"I know keep going."

They traveled two or three miles. "You see that big boulder sticking out up there? Slow down, and go around it ."

The snow mobile came to a crawl.

She steered them alongside the rock wall.

Everything was white.

It was hard to make out what was what.

Her body ached.

She was sure she was close to being frozen.

"See those branches hanging down?"

"Yes."

"Stop there."

She pulled under the branches and turned off the engine.

Mark climbed off the back and moved several out of the way.

The mouth of a large cave came into view.

"Wow, I couldn't even tell it was here." She said.

"How did you know it was here."

"Grey and I used to hunt a lot, whenever I was stateside."

"He had too much whiskey and broke his leg falling out of a deer stand. We both had to hole up here and ride out the storm. We found it by accident to find shelter."

"Pull Inside."

Once the snowmobile and sled were inside the entrance, Mark unloaded the supplies.

He filled the little pot with snow and re-covered the entrance behind them.

He built a small fire and heated the water.

Megan sat down on the ground, she was exhausted.

Once the soup was ready he handed her a cup.

 "I don't want it. I just want to go to sleep."

"Well, I need you to drink it."

 He said, sternly. He didn't like her color.

"Let me help you with your boots."

 He reached down and pulled one off.

"Why are your feet wet? You're socks are soaked too."

"The snow was wet yesterday, and they never dried. It was too cold."

Her face was flushed.

"Come on drink this soup for me."

He made a pallet out of the camping mats and some of the blankets, making sure the cold ground could not be felt through them.

The cave was starting to warm up.

"Come lay over here."

Megan reluctantly got up.

"Your shirt is wet too." This was not good.

He helped her out of her shirt bra and pants.

She lay down. He felt her skin.

Her forehead was hot. The rest of her was ice cold.

Mark retrieved two Tylenol from the first aid kit, and gave them to her.

She took them without complaint.

He covered her top half and rubbed her feet and legs gently until they warmed up a bit.

He hung her clothes on the sled in front of the fire to dry them.

He checked his bandage.

There was a small amount of blood on it.

It would hold until tomorrow.

After more wood was put on the fire, he laid down next her, and wrapped his warm body around hers.

He fell asleep listening to the howling wind.

THE DISC

James rubbed his hands together.

He had waited an hour for the wind to let up, wondering if they had noticed him missing.

It took him 20 additional minutes to hot wire the snow mobile.

He thought of the men's bodies in the snow.

He didn't call any of them friends, but he said a small prayer for them.

This was how she cared for her followers.

It took him 4 hours to reach the ranger station.

He had hoped the man and girl would be there, but it was empty.

He could tell someone had been there.

By the look of the blood spots on the floor he assumed it was them.

He built a small fire with the wood that had been left behind.

James removed his boots and socks, and hung them over the chair to dry.

Once the beef jerky he had found in the cabin was gone he had no other plan, except to get through till spring, and somehow take the disc and expose the cult.

He dropped to his knees and prayed for God to forgive him for being led astray, and for Mark and Megan's safety.

Once he had made a pallet on the floor he was asleep in minutes.

Hours later, the men circled the Ranger station.

There were four of them. Zack slowly opened the door.

Paul studied the sleeping man on the floor.

He looked over at Zack.

"Kill him." He whispered.

He watched as Zack reached down, and in an instant snapped James's neck.

A loud crash woke Mark.

He jumped up, naked with nothing but his weapon.

He moved towards the entrance.

A large branch had fallen off the massive tree.

He waited a few minutes to make sure there was nothing else.

He dressed and went outside to pee, and gather snow to melt, for coffee, and soup.

The storm was howling.

He drank the coffee standing up, readjusted the branches at the entrance, and slipped back in behind Megan.

He put his arms around her and pulled her to him.

She was limp and burning up.

Her breathing slow and shallow.

"Megan." He said loudly giving her a shake.

She did not respond. He shook her harder, still nothing.

Covering her, he built a larger fire. The cave soon became very warm.

Mark placed a pack under her feet.

It would alleviate shock symptoms, and help protect the internal organs.

Her entire body started to jerk violently.

She was having a seizure.

Fever induced he assumed.

He removed the pack and rolled her on her side, cradling her head in his lap to keep her from injury.

The seizure lasted two or three minutes.

It seemed like an eternity.

When it was over he pulled her closer to check for breathing.

Nothing.

He checked her pulse. It was faint.

Mark plugged her nose and gave her two quick breaths.

He could feel panic rising. Still nothing.

His heart hammered in his chest. He tried again.

Suddenly she started coughing.

He rolled her onto her side. Her cough subsided, she lay still.

She was breathing regularly, although she had a wheeze.

He ran his hands through his hair. "Jesus Christ," he said quietly.

Mark felt like he was going to hyperventilate.

His palms were sweating. He leaned back against the cave wall, pulling Megan into his lap stroking her hair, humming to himself.

He didn't know what tune it was.

Something he had heard as a kid. It calmed him.

What the hell was he thinking bringing her to this God forsaken Mountain. This was no place for someone like her.

It was too harsh, too desolate. Tears rolled down his cheeks.

 He wiped them with his sleeve, pulling her closer.

"Don't you leave me Megan, don't you do it."

He held her through the night.

He was afraid to go to sleep.

He worried that she would have another seizure and stop breathing again.

He made several trips to the fire to keep it going.

The next day came and went.

He thought of her dying and decided if she did, he would let the fire die out.

Then he would sit until he died too. It was the only way.

Thanksgiving came and went without his knowledge.

He crushed antibiotics and spoon fed them to her, mixed with water.

She didn't open her eyes but she had no trouble swallowing.

Two days later she opened her eyes for brief moments.

The blizzard raged on, outside. It was all good and well.

They were unable to travel like this anyway.

He paced the cave.

He had studied the map so much he knew it by heart.

Frustration was beginning to build. Four days had gone by.

He was sat and held her, as the sun went down on another day.

Looking down at her face he was grateful for the time they had spent together.

He was glad that he had fallen in love.

Glad for all of it. He had no regrets.

Megan had turned his life around.

The things he thought mattered really didn't.

He was ready for any war, but he sure hadn't been ready for her.

He bent down and kissed her forehead.

"Please come back to me…" He was at his wit's end.

He wiped his eyes, and saw her looking at him.

"What happened?" she said.

"You tried to check out on me." His heart pounded.

He hugged her too him.

"Is there any food?"

He starred at her and laughed. Unbelievable, he thought smiling.

She ate two soup pouches and a pack of beef jerky.

He told her about the seizure, and his last few days.

GREY

Two days later mark decided they couldn't wait anymore.

She was coughing like crazy and the antibiotics were almost gone.

He knew there were more at the cabin.

Mark also wanted to get the second snow mobile.

The rest if the trip was a steep ride, straight up the Teton Mountain range.

He didn't know if one snow mobile would carry them both that far.

He didn't want to take a chance, getting stranded with her still sick.

It would be a long trip for her, but she had already told him that she wasn't staying behind in the cave.

Besides he couldn't drive both snow mobiles.

They left out, heading south.

Mark drove until he reached the tree line, of the Ranger station.

He stopped, something was off.

Mark pulled out his binoculars, and spotted the snow mobile.

He was sure it was his.

There was no movement from the small building the door stood open.

He told Megan to stay put.

"Don't leave me," she pleaded.

"He walked to her and pulled her close to him." Babe, I love you.

"I'll be back. I swear. You stay put."

He cocked his weapon and seconds later he was gone.

She saw him emerge again, from the side of the building.

Megan watched him through the binoculars.

He went inside. She held her breath.

Moments later he emerged. He was moving fast.

She saw him start the Snowmobile and drive towards her.

"What's going on?"

"I'll explain later."

"Aren't we heading to the cabin?"

"Yes. Get on." His original plan had been to leave her at the ranger station.

Now he could not.

The body inside had been mauled by wolves from the looks of The Tracks. There was no hiding it.

He would leave her at the tree line and walk in.

Mark felt his breast pocket.

The disc was safely inside, He wondered what was on it, and if the man had died for it.

Two hours later the cabin came into sight.

Before Megan could argue he put his mouth on hers and kissed her.

He mouthed, "Love you," and like a flash was gone.

The cabin was empty and he returned shortly Antibiotics in tow.

They started up the snowmobiles and headed north.

Four hours later they crossed the Wyoming / Idaho pass, across the pavement and back into the woods.

Another four or five miles, Mark spotted a stone column and turned right.

It was a bumpy Ride, the snow had accumulated.

A mile down the drive they came to a huge iron gate.

It was attached on both sides to a large 12 foot stone wall, with barbed wire on top.

He looked at the security camera and pushed the button.

"What's the password Asshole."

The deep voice resonated out of the speaker.

"Black Crow."

"Wrong, I changed it."

Mark shook his head in annoyance. The large Gate swung open with a groan.

They pulled in, and headed up to the house.

Greydon Stark waited at the door for them.

The two men embraced and slapped each other on the back.

"Good to see you man." Grey said.

"Ma'am" He tipped his hat.

He was a giant of a man. Six foot nine.

He towered over Mark. He wore his black Hair long in a braid that hung down his back.

A young man scurried out to get the bags.

Mark guessed he was 22 or so.

He was small dark hair wiry type.

"That's carl. Good kid, Picked him up a few months back. He's ok."

Carl unloaded their bags and brought them inside.

"I was wondering when you were gonna get here."

"Thought you got your Ass shot off."

"I did." Mark lifted his shirt."

Grey stepped closer, and lifted the bandage.

"Damn son, looks like shit."

"Thanks."

Grey had grown a thick goatee since Mark had last seen him.

"Who is the lovely Lady?" he asked.

"I'm Megan," she said shaking his large hand.

He gave Mark a curious look.

"Good to meet you." He said.

"There's food in there on the stove."

They headed inside. He fixed them both a plate.

Pork chops and potatoes, and Green beans.

Megan felt like she was in heaven.

After dinner Megan laid down on the small sofa while Mark and Grey took a walk.

"That's quite a story," Grey said after he had filled him in.

"Where do you go from here, you can't run forever."

"I know. I have to get her out of these mountains. She's sick. Pneumonia I suspect. I just need to keep her safe."

Grey studied Mark, as he handed him a mug of coffee.

He shook his head.

"No way, you fell for her. You know better. We don't get involved. You of all People should know that."

"I know, but it's too late I love her."

"That's dangerous shit. Have you forgotten about Molly and the baby?"

"No, I haven't forgotten. How could I forget that." He glanced at the small picture Frame on the table.

He remembered all too well, watching them drive away to the safe house.

The leak had to have been internal.

There was no other possibility. They never made it.

They found them on the road, but it was too late.

Molly's throat had been cut from ear to ear.

The baby's too. It had also been winter then.

Mark remembered Molly's red hair mixing with the Blood and the snow.

Grey had fallen to his knees, screaming, Cursing God, and himself.

They had both walked away from the agency after that.

Mark helped Grey build his fortress and then he had disappeared into the wind.

"They died because of what we do. Don't you ever forget that."

"I won't. This is not the same. I was hired to protect her. It just happened."

"I get it. I do." He shook his head.

"Look at her. She's a fine woman."

He meant it.

"Stay here for a while. We'll figure something out. I guess I can't blame you. I didn't try to fall in love with Molly either. She just snatched me up."

Mark laughed.

He remembered Grey had asked her out for weeks before she would go on one date with him.

Grey glanced at the picture.

He could still remember how her hair smelled of Lilac, and the feel of the babies red curls.

He sighed.

Those ghosts were better left for another time.

"I spent years blaming myself. Holing up here. Now I realize they are events beyond our control. I'm not sorry I loved her." Grey said, as he picked up the small frame.

"You're in too deep now. There's no going back. So we gotta fight. Hell, I'm in, got nothing else to do. I need to do more research on these assholes." Grey stood, his head nearly hitting the ceiling.

"But it won't be tonight. I'm gonna turn in." he gently placed the picture back on the table.

"You can have the bedroom down the hall. It has its own bathroom, for the little lady."

He raised his pinky up in the air jokingly.

Mark punched him in the arm.

"Dickhead."

He woke Megan and steered her to the bedroom. He helped her with her heavy sweater like a child.

Mark slipped one of his clean white t-shirts over her head.

She got into the bed, and he covered her with the heavy quilts.

"Is it safe?"

"Yes, Baby....it's safe, go to sleep."

He kissed her forehead.

Mark knew this constant running was no life for her.

Something Grey had said made him feel better though.

They were not responsible for evil. They could only do, all they could to keep the ones they loved safe.

He unbuttoned his Flannel Shirt, and took off the thermal one underneath.

After a long hot shower, he slipped on a t shirt, and a pair of sweats.

He starred out of the thick paned window, Bullet proof glass.

The snow was still falling. For once he was sick of it.

He was warm for the first time in weeks, yet he found no comfort.

The house was silent.

Mark opened the door and listened.

He heard Grey's loud snore's coming from down the hall.

He locked the door and pulled out his lap top.

He inserted the disc and waited. The screen lit up.

The sick bastards even had their own logo

A black and grey rainbow, with a double headed serpent crawling through.

He clicked on the members icon.

It was a complete log of all 6343 members.

The disc also contained detailed financial records, bank account numbers and transactions, as well as a list of numerical codes.

It looked like most of the contributions had come from campaign funds, and Politicians.

This ran deeper that he suspected.

There was also a list of targets. People that had been hit and people still to be eliminated.

It was detailed log on who had traded what.

This was the trump card he had been waiting for.

He reached his bag, and retrieved a flash drive, and a blank disc.

Then he carefully peeled the label off the disc, and stuck it to the blank one.

He placed the real disc in his bag, and put the blank one under his pillow.

The flash drive stayed in his pocket. He slid into bed next to Megan.

He thought of jack and wondered what he would do in this situation. He pulled Megan into his arms.

Kissing her, and hugging her tightly to him. She snuggled in his arms. Sleep eventually came.

Megan woke up early. Mark slept.

She took a much needed shower. Her bones ached.

She felt like she would never be well again.

This Infection or whatever it was continued dragging on and on.

She grabbed her antibiotic and headed to the kitchen.

Grey looked up from the kitchen table. She was a sight.

She wore a pink flannel shirt, her long dark hair hung loosely down her back to her waist.

"Coffee?"

"Yes please."

She took the cup and sipped on it, sliding into the barstool across from Grey.

He knew why Mark had fallen for her. Hell, who wouldn't.

She was dainty, with beautiful features big eyes and full red lips.

Grey almost felt ashamed.

He needed to call that woman in town.

It had been too long.

He saw Marge from time to time, when he was lonely.

It was a mutual thing.

They both wanted sex, and companionship when it was convenient.

Megan smiled uncomfortably, while Grey starred.

"I'm sorry," he said I was lost in my thoughts.

" I wasn't trying to be rude. It's been a long time since I've seen a beautiful woman."

Grey got up and fried bacon and eggs.

She ate two plates by the time Mark came out.

He smiled and leaned in to Mark, "That one can eat."

Nodding towards Megan.

"Thanks that was so good. I never want to see another MRE."

"How long have you lived out here?"

"Oh about 10 years, since my family was killed."

He pointed to the picture on the table of Molly and Hannah.

"They were beautiful." She stated.

"Yes, they were."

He starred at the photo.

"It doesn't really bother me to talk about it now."

He poured another cup of coffee and refilled hers.

He came back and sat down next to Mark.

Mark and I were on assignment.

We were tracking a government assassin.

The entire operation was compromised.

There were threats made against my family and the two of us.

There must have been an internal leak, because during the course of transporting my family to the safe house, they were killed Mark and I found them on the road.

My Molly had her throat cut and little Hannah, his voice cracked..hers too.

They were left in the snow, on the road.

"I am so sorry. I can't even imagine your pain."

She went to him and hugged him.

She realized why Mark was so overprotective and why he had fought their relationship so desperately.

"Well life goes on." Grey said.

"Would you like to see the horses?"

He asked, trying to lighten the mood.

"I would love to. We had horses at home. My father raised Thoroughbred's. We have quite a few."

She was excited the horses reminded her of home.

The entire property was fenced in with a huge stone Wall surrounding it.

It reminded Megan of a medieval castle.

There was even a watch tower made of the same stone.

The path led to the back of the house and into the stables.

The familiar smell of hay, and manure made her inhale deeply.

It gave her comfort.

Carl was working in the Barn.

Grey called him over to meet Megan.

"This is carl."

He works for me.

Carl stopped dead in his tracks. He looked at Megan as if he had seen a Ghost.

He backed up and stammered that he had something to do.

Mark starred at Grey.

"He's a kid. Relax. Don't kill him just yet."

He knew that crazed look.

Megan had worked her way into the stalls.

There were five horses in all.

Two stallions, one palomino, a quarter Horse and a massive Arabian named Klondike.

"They are beautiful."

"Yes they are." Grey said.

They have gotten me through some rough times."

"I'll bet. Some people say horses are very therapeutic."

She replied, caressing the horse's neck.

"They are, but not as therapeutic as Jim Beam."

Grey said with a grin.

Grey sent Carl to exercise Klondike, after breakfast.

Megan was feeling poorly again, and decided to nap.

Grey locked the house down. There would be no getting in.

If the Perimeter was even breached, an alarm would sound that could be heard for miles.

Mark made sure Carl didn't have a key.

He still didn't like the way he had looked at her when they met.

Mark had not taken his eyes off of her.

It pissed him off that Grey took him at face value.

Grey and Mark took the horses out.

The snow flew in tiny flurries around them.

It had been two weeks since they arrived at Grey's.

The horses walked slowly. Snow crunching beneath their feet.

"Maybe you should take the disc to the papers. Get it published."

"That oughta ruin the party."

"Does your friend still work at the paper?"

"Yes she does. I need to go and see her anyway. If you know what I mean."

"One of us is going to have to go to town and talk to her."

"I don't have a phone. Haven't had one in years, and I don't wanna use the short wave radio. Too many Ears listening."

"We can't use the pass. It's still snowed in. The best way would be on horseback or wait till spring."

"Spring is a long way out."

"Then I guess were riding cross country."

"Megan can't make that trip. I can't put her back out there, but I can't leave her here. She's still sick. She's just not bouncing back. She has lost weight."

"Megan does look pale." Grey stated.

"I'm not leaving her here that's all I know. I don't want any more surprises."

"If they found the cabin, they will find this place too."

Christmas came and went.

Mark gave Megan a small ring he had bought from Grey.

Time seemed to be standing still.

Mark and Grey spent the mornings researching the cult, and taking care of the horses, and in the evening they all ate together.

Mark took her on a few midnight rides, when the weather permitted.

Grey tried out all his recipes he had conjured up over the years.

He was glad for the company.

It was like having a family again.

The nights belonged to Mark and Megan.

They made love almost every night.

He was beside himself with love for her.

His life had a purpose, a meaning, he felt like he finally belonged somewhere.

The next morning, Grey stormed into the Kitchen.

"The Kid didn't come back last night."

"Where did he go?"

"He said he was taking a walk. I get up this morning and the Quarter horse is gone. Saddle too." Grey complained.

"I told you that little bastard couldn't be trusted. I will tear his liver out if he brings them down on us."

"I need you to do me a favor." Mark said.

"Besides housing you, and cooking my fingers to the bone?"

"You love cooking for me."

"I'm yanking your balls." Grey replied.

"I need you to get the story out."

Grey shook his head

"Understood. I'll go to town. I'll ride thunder. Get Marge to run the story. I should hit town in two days. I need a break from you two anyway. All that " smoochie-smoochie", makin' me sick."

Mark laughed. "Alright then Old timer."

They worked out the last details, and packed up the horse.

Within an hour Grey was on his way.

He had given him the disc. He hadn't told him about the flash drive.

He just couldn't take the chance.

LOVES GIFT

Megan's fever came back that night.

She had finished the antibiotics.

He gave her the last of the Tylenol. Her fever persisted into the night.

First light he was taking her to town.

He could make good time. He would try to catch up with Grey.

He left hay for the Horses and filled the trough.

He loaded the pack, at first light. Helped her get dressed, and wrapped a wool scarf around her head.

He lifted her into the saddle, so he could hold onto her.

By late evening he had picked up Grey's tracks.

By now he had hit the main trail. The moon was full so he rode on into the night.

By first light he had caught up with Grey.

Megan had talked a little but slept most of the trip.

Her body heat kept him warm. Grey led him to the little clinic. There was no hospital.

Mark led him into the door. Doctor Morgan listened to her lungs.

He asked Mark a series of questions. He drew blood, and inserted an I.V.

She needs fluids, and the x ray showed she has pneumonia. Mark explained that she had already taken antibiotics.

He prescribed a different medicine and gave her a shot of penicillin.

After two hours Megan was still asleep.

"It's normal," the doctor explained. "Her body was going through a lot."

He told Mark not to worry. "I will send enough samples with you to get her back on her feet. Keep her hydrated, and don't worry, the meds I prescribed won't hurt the Baby. I've given her something to help her rest tonight."

"Baby?" mark stuttered.

"Yes. You didn't know your wife is having a baby?"

"No." he said in a small voice.

"Well," Dr. Morgan slapped him on the back. "Congratulations. They will be fine."

Mark stood dumbfounded, staring at the doctor.

"You can take your wife to the little hotel next door. I'll come check on her tomorrow. I think you'll see a big difference."

Everything was moving in slow motion.

He walked out, grateful for the blast of cool air.

Mark carried her across the street, to the motel.

Grey had already rented two rooms. The doctor had put the horses up for the night.

He was also the town vet.

He helped her into the bed, and walked Grey outside.

"What did the doctor say?"

"He said she has pneumonia. He gave her fluids. He says she will be ok."

He didn't think it was right for him to tell anyone before Megan knew.

"That's good. I'm heading to Marge's. I'm gonna make sure she prints that story, and I'm going to get laid. It's been way too long."

He grinned and slapped Mark on the back.

Mark closed the door behind him and looked at Megan lying on the bed.

His eyes traveled to her stomach.

He was going to be a father. She was the mother of his child.

It was unbelievable.

He dried his eyes. He sat down on the bed and took her hand to his lips, gently kissing her fingers.

"I love you baby."

He woke up at 4am.

It was time for her medicine.

He woke her up. She sat up on the side of the bed with her eyes closed.

"I gotta pee."

He helped her to the bathroom.

She was definitely under the influence.

She stripped off her clothes and got into the shower.

Mark smiled as he turned on the water and did the best he could, while she stood with her eyes closed.

Mark dried her, and tucked her back into bed.

He showered, and put on his shorts.

"Alright. Goodnight." He said with a smile as he slid in next to her.

He moved his hand over her stomach. He felt a little bump there.

He hadn't noticed it before.

He fell asleep quickly.

The next morning he was watching Tv when Megan woke up.

"Oh my god I'm starving."

"Well, good morning to you, babe." He smiled.

"I didn't think I was going to make it. I couldn't breathe, it hurt to cough. Then next thing I know I wake up at the clinic and now here." She was back.

"You were pretty out of it. I was worried."

He touched her face.

"There is one more thing, I have to tell you."

"What?" she looked at him, and saw the serious look on his face.

"What?.... Mark?" she started to panic.

"Well honey I don't quite know how to tell you this, but you are going to have a baby."

She starred at him.

"What are you talking about?"

"You are pregnant. The doctor said so."

She looked down at her stomach.

"Oh my god....We are going to be parents."

Her eyes filled with tears.

"I don't know if I can do this right now. I'm scared. We are running for our lives."

He held both her hands.

"We can, and we will. I will be with you every step of the way. Don't be scared."

He pulled her into his arms and kissed her gently.

The Beginning of the End

Anita paced the floor

"Priestess."

"Did you find my daughter?"

"No, but we located James. We tracked him to the old Ranger station."

"Did you see any sign of Megan?"

"No ma'am , But we finished James."

"Did you search him?"

"No- you didn't tell us to."

"Idiots, he downloaded our files. There are important people that don't want their Identities revealed, People in the public eye. He can take us all down with this Disc."

She opened the door, the snow was relentless.

She felt like the whole thing was slipping out of her fingers.

"Get me Ethan on the phone. I want to know if he has a connection at the CIA."

They sat in the diner and ate breakfast.

"Marge is running the story." Grey said.

"Good maybe this will give us the edge we need. Where is the disc?"

"I gave it to Marge."

"You gave her the disc." Mark said dryly.

He was getting annoyed, although Grey didn't know he had the flash drive.

He wasn't thinking.

"I'll get it back." Grey said defensively.

"Don't be so sure. You don't know who is involved."

Grey slammed his money down and went to the motel.

The Job wouldn't be complete, without an argument.

Every job they had worked on together, ended the same way.

Two days later the story hit the papers.

In the next few days the FBI arrested hundreds of members.

Grey was overjoyed. Mark not so much.

He tried to explain to Grey that there were over six thousand members, and that this was only a drop in the bucket.

Grey did give him the disc back, with a smug look.

Staying put was getting under Mark's skin.

The next day they arrested two hundred more. It was a start.

Mark and Megan had a quiet dinner and retreated to the Motel.

Grey had company in his room for the night. Marge had brought a bottle of Champagne.

Megan and Mark showered, and made love, he was trying to be gentle, he didn't understand all the baby business, and what would be safe.

Megan assured him that it was fine.

After they showered again, and broke out the snacks they had bought earlier that day.

Since she had gotten pregnant he swore he had gained weight.

Mark sat down on the bed next to Megan.

"I was thinking…..Let's get married, as soon as this is over.

I love you. I want to marry you. I want our baby to have a real family."

She touched his face. "Yes. I would love to marry you."

That was all Mark heard, when the windows exploded

LOSS

It was touch and go the first few days.

The nurses weren't sure if Mark would live or die.

His head injury was severe.

His brain was swollen. The Doctor's sedated him so he could heal.

Slowly the swelling went down. Seven days later he opened his eyes.

There was something in his nose. The room didn't look familiar.

He reached up to rip it out. A face appeared above him

"Hi." She said as she guided his arms back to his side.

"I'm Kristi , Your nurse."

"What's going on where am I? Where's Megan?"

"You are in the hospital."

"How long have I been here?" He started to sit up but the tubes and wires prevented it.

"You were in an explosion, and shot several times, you sustained a head injury, and have been here for seven days." She said in a kind voice.

"Oh, my god, seven days."

There was no telling what had happened to Megan.

"I need to find her. I have to get out of here."

He was working himself into a Frenzy.

The last thing he remembered was an explosion, and something about Grey, but he couldn't quite wrap his mind around it.

Kristi felt bad for him. "I don't know who Megan is but I'll see what I can find out." She was blond and thin. Her voice was soft and soothing.

"She's my wife. I have to know where she is….." His voice trailed off as he faded in and out.

"You need to rest." She said softly, as she injected pain medicine into his IV.

He drifted off again.

Kristi asked around the hospital if anyone else had been brought in with him.

No had seen anyone else. If there was, the nurses would know it. They knew all the comings and goings of the hospital. Nurses had a unique communication system. If it happened they would know.

The nurses also had a special interest in Mark.

He was handsome, and rugged and a mystery.

A few days later, two men from the Idaho state police came to see Mark.

Officer Johns and Parker introduced themselves and began to question him.

"Why were you at the Motel."

"Where is Megan?" Mark asked.

They continued to ask him questions and he continued to repeat himself.

He wasn't answering anything until he got some information.

The two men finally gave up, threatening to He had been in a few prison camps, and in comparison their interrogation skills were mediocre. They finally left, threatening to return the next day. Kristi entered the room and insisted they leave.

"I checked around, you were brought in alone. There have been a lot of cops swarming around. I know you're not under arrest, but they definitely want you for something. A FBI guy has been coming around."

"Thanks." Mark was grateful for any information.

She put medicine in his IV and the last thing he remembered before he passed out was a man flashing a badge.

The next time he woke up, two armed guards were sitting in his room and third man in a suit, sat next to his bed.

"Hello," he said politely. "I'm Tom Dane, FBI. He was a tall man six foot two, bald, with bright blue eyes.

He had to be in his late forty's. He held his Stetson in his hand.

"You're not an easy man to find. Tell me about the cult."

"What happened to the woman I was with?"

"I don't know."

Mark laid back and sighed.

"What brings the FBI?"

"I think you know."

"I need to know what you know about Anita Goldman, and the Cult."

He gave him a basic run down of what he knew. He told him about Jack and Megan and how he had been hired to guard her.

How she had gotten sick and that they had taken the disc to the paper.

"I know that a big chunk of the cult was disbanded, after the article. We are looking for Anita."

Mark had one memory.

He had asked her to marry him.

When the room exploded, he had seen a flash of Greys giant frame, rushing into the room and carrying Megan out.

"I don't know about your friend, or your wife. There were no other people found. There are mass graves. The lower members were murdered to keep them from talking. I'm going tomorrow. There are two new sites."

Tom crossed the room and showed Mark photos of excavation sites.

"The first site was only Men. I have their pictures. I can show you."

"I want to be there." Mark stated. "You can get me released."

"You aren't ready to be discharged."

"I'm leaving here tomorrow with or without you." Mark said.

"Alright then. I'll see what I can do. I'm catching shit for the guards anyway."

He handed Mark his Pack.

Inside were his guns his ammo and bundles of cash, his laptop, and all his other belongings.

"Where did you get that?"

"Evidence."

"Ahh well..." Mark shrugged.

"I'll see you tomorrow. Try to stay alive."

"I'll be ready. I have to find her. I've lost too much time already."

Tom tipped his Stetson to the nurses and walked out.

Tom was late. He probably wasn't coming. Mark was getting annoyed.

Kristi had told him that the guards were gone.

Mark pulled out his IV. He used the pole to get onto his feet.

He walked unsteadily to the closet, and got his clothes and boots.

It was a chore to put them on. He looked out the door. Kristi was coming down the hall. There was no way around her.

He was standing in the room when she walked in.

She starred at him, sighing, hands on her hips.

"Where do you think you are going?"

"I have to find her. I can't stay here." He said.

"She means everything to me. She is pregnant for god's sake. I have to know."

Kristi shook her head. "At least let me change your bandage."

She came back a few moments later, with a bag of bandages and gauze.

"I'll be here the next few days, If you need help. The guards are still gone."

"That's not good. They are coming for me."

"I have an idea." Kristi ran out of the room and came back moments later with a wheelchair, and several blankets.

'Sit down.' She covered him up with the blankets, wrapping the last one around his head while pushing him out the door, heading for the service elevator.

He held his bag in his lap. Once they exited the side entrance he stood, and thanked her. He called Tom Dane from her cell phone.

She went inside, as he walked away. Kristi would miss him. She wished she could find a love like that.

As he suspected Tom had not pulled the guards off. For some reason he trusted him.

He knew checked the disc to see if Tom was on it, and he wasn't. Mark wasn't surprised, but there would be no more mistakes.

His wound was bleeding again. He stopped in the bathroom of the Mc Donald's and changed it. When he came outside Tom was waiting in his truck.

He got in and they drove off, quickly. Tom handed him a coffee, and a sausage biscuit.

"Guess I'm stuck with you for a while."

"Looks that way." Marks stomach hurt. His nerves were going haywire. They drove 40 miles to the first dig.

"We got a lot of work to do. After the next dig we'll meet up with my team. I've got a few good guys working with me."

"Are you sure they can be trusted." mark asked.

"I'd bet my life on it."

THE DIG

Mark gritted his teeth, and prayed that he would not find her like this. He searched his memory.

When he saw Grey running with her she had been alive…hadn't she?

They pulled into the site.

It was a densely wooded area. Mark was surprised by the number of people that we're working together.

There were more bodies than he could count. They were lined up and covered. He lifted the drape off each one of them. His heart lurching every time, knowing it could be her, or Grey.

His hands were shaking. He felt shaky on the inside as well.

It was almost too much to bear.

He walked over to the tent, where Tom stood, talking to the volunteers.

"She's not here. Neither is Grey."

"Glad to hear it. You want to look at the Photo's? I had them brought over. They are from all the victims that we've found so far"

Mark shook his Head, and sat down in the Lawnchair.

His legs felt like rubber. He felt like the carpet could get pulled out from under him at any moment.

Mark looked through the Photo's. There were men and women, even a child. There were over a hundred.

Megan and Grey weren't among the dead.

His stomach was twisted into tight knots.

Not knowing how he would react if he found her dead.

He guessed he would snap. Go right off the deep end.

But on this day, she was safe in his memory.

After the second dig, Mark asked to be dropped off at a motel.

The day had just been too much. His emotions were shot to hell. Tom didn't think it was a good idea, but Mark insisted.

He promised to come back for him the next day.

They said their goodbye's.

Mark sat down on the bed, His hands in his lap.

He had lost her.

He had to find her, dead or alive and bring her home.

He knew the odds. It had been nine days.

It pissed him off that people were just moving on with their lives.

If it were up to him he would stop everything, until she was found and the world was right again. He was exhausted.

Mark had lost a fair amount of blood. The bandage had soaked through for a third time.

He didn't give a shit.

He lay across the bed and wept.

He called Kristi the next morning.

He started running a fever.

She brought him more bandages, and a lengthy lecture.

In the end she convinced him to stay put, saying that he would be no good to Megan if he was dead.

His three days turned into five.

Tom checked on him several times. His nurse checked on him every day.

A week later the wound had finally closed up, and he was feeling better.

He called Tom, to come back and pick him up. He felt like he was just going through the motions.

The shear surrealness was unbearable.

It made him sad that he was getting used to looking at dead bodies.

It was a nightmare. Once they covered all the sites, he had Tom take him to Grey's.

He fed the horses and Tom promised to come back up a few times a week to tend to them.

They had searched the computer for Anita, but she had also vanished off the face of the earth.

Mark was pissed off that he was weak and had no stamina. His injuries had taken a toll on him.

He went back to town with a photo of Megan he had printed off the computer.

It was a picture of her in front of her father's house, for an article.

Mark stopped at the diner where they had eaten their last dinner together.

The motel across the street was demolished and what was left still had yellow crime tape around it.

He showed the picture to everyone he saw. No one remembered seeing her.

The days dragged on and on, with no luck no breaks….just nothing.

FALLING

Six months had passed since that fateful night at the motel.

Mark stood on the porch of the cabin, and watched the sun set. His face was hard.

Dark circles had formed under his eyes.

He had grown a full beard, and his hair was long and scraggly. It was a shear lack of caring.

It was late June. The mountains were unseasonably warm for this time of year.

He glanced at the field full of wildflowers. Megan would have loved them.

He sipped his coffee and sat down in the old rocker. It creaked under his weight.

In his mind he had gone over it a thousand times.

She had been alive.

He remembered throwing himself over her as the glass shattered. Men had come into the room, he couldn't remember how many.

Six, maybe seven. Grey had appeared in the doorway.

He remembered getting shot the first time. Then everything had exploded.

Grey had carried Megan out. That was all.

Tom had sent him to hypnosis to remember that much.

He had searched for 6 months.

The hospitals, the Morgue's the newspapers, all the small towns around.

There was nothing. No trail.

It had all gone cold.

Finally he returned to the cabin. It was the place he felt closest to her.

Here where their love had begun.

When he first arrived he would walk the fields, till dark.

Then just sleep wherever he ended up.

The FBI had stayed in contact for the first few months, but now no one came, except Tom.

He dropped in from time to time. Usually to tell him of new bodies being found.

Mark had provided DNA from both Megan and Greys hairbrushes.

He could not go to one more dig. He was done.

Mark started to gather fire wood. The winter would be coming soon.

The breeze blew, and he thought he caught a scent of her perfume.

He closed his eyes, and thought of all the times they had made love.

He remembered the way her lips felt on his, and the softness of her. The wind blew again, and the sweet smell was gone.

There had never been a woman like her and there would be no other. Not for him.

The thought of the baby made him ache inside. He put his hand over his heart and rubbed, hoping to ease the pain just a little.

Mark had frequented the bar as of late.

The Golden cue was a hole in the wall.

He drank till the numbness set in.

It lessened the ache.

He couldn't live with the fact that he had failed her.

Loving her had made him careless.

Not that he was sorry for it, he just knew he had lost his sense of duty.

Out in the Jeep he finished the bottle of Jim beam.

He drove to the cabin and loaded the 9mm.

Tonight the pain would end for him.

He couldn't go on without her.

There was nothing left.

He pressed the nine to his temple.

"Forgive me, God, I just can't be without her."

The weapon Jammed.

Mark pulled the trigger again. Still Jammed.

In a rage he pointed it to the ceiling, and squeezed.

Three rounds fired into the ceiling.

He set the gun on the table, and stepped back dumbfounded.

He remembered what Grey used to say.

A bullet never lies.

It wasn't his time. He rushed to the sink, as the Jim beam came up.

Once his stomach settled he knew what he had to do.

He had to find her and bring her home.

He would bury her in the field where the Wildflowers bloomed.

He guessed God expected him to do this, and live out his years.

Mark was on the edge.

He would do his best to carry out his new plan.

THE GIFT

He heard the truck before he saw it.

He grabbed the 9mm, off the table and stepped back on the porch.

Tom Dane stepped out.

"Christ, You look like shit."

Mark starred at him.

"I have news."

"Tell me." His heart began to race.

"I found Grey."

"Where, in a dig?"

"No, in a hospital in Idaho."

Mark's hair stood up on his arms. He jumped up out of the rocker.

"He's alive?"

"Yes. In coma but alive. They thought he was a homeless person, when he was brought in. The local police confirmed it. They never looked any further."

"What about Megan?"

Tom shook his head.

"Just him."

"I'm heading over in the morning to look at the surveillance.

I thought you may want to come along. Give me a positive I.D."

He didn't need it.

He had already ran the DNA, there was no doubt, but he felt like Mark was at the end.

He needed this. "Yeah."

"Good, let's go get a drink."

Mark sighed. His stomach churned from the Jim Beam he had just thrown up.

They sat at the bar and talked.

Mark felt more normal than he had in weeks.

They drank whiskey. Tom was a good man.

Mark was glad Grey had been found. He needed answers.

A busty blond, who Mark recognized as a regular came over, and sat next to him.

"I've been watching you."

"Yeah?" mark replied.

"I can see you are in some sort of pain."

Mark sighed and gave no response.

"I can make it all better. I know what you need."

She ran her hand up his leg.

He turned and looked at her. She was a nice looking woman, blond with big breasts.

"What do you think I need?"

"You need good loving."

"Is that right?" He was drunk. He knew it. It felt good to have a woman touch him. It had been a long time.

"Why don't you take me home, and I'll make you feel a whole lot better."

She rubbed his shoulder and massive arms. Mark ran his fingers through his hair.

"I don't think so." He got up threw money on the bar.

Tom followed and they started to walk away.

"Hey" she yelled at him.

"How are you gonna disrespect me like that." He turned, and kept walking.

She followed him and slapped him in the back of the head.

He turned. "No Disrespect intended." He said, and continued to walk.

Tom turned. He was drunk. Very drunk.

"With all due respect lady you are a slut, and he doesn't want to fuck you."

He slapped Mark on the back, and laughed like a hyena.

As they walk out, her boyfriend Sid walked up and smacked Mark in the back of the head.

Mark turned expecting the blond again.

"Is there a problem?" Sid said.

"Not unless you want to make one."

"Well, maybe I don't like the way you talking to my lady."

Mark smiled.

"That's no lady." Tom declared, as he staggered away.

Mark felt anger well up in him. He hadn't felt anything in months.

"You may be a big guy, but I ain't worried about you." Sid said.

"The bigger they are the harder they fall." someone sneered from the crowd.

Several of Sid's friends had gathered. Sid punched Mark square in the face.

Mark stared at him. He stood like stone.

It had been a while.

He hit Sid one time and knocked him out.

"Anyone else got a problem with me?" he asked.

The crowd quickly dispersed.

He walked out and found Tom puking along the side of the Jeep.

"You better be done." he told him don't puke in my Jeep.

"You gonna shoot me if I do?"

Mark shook his head.

"I should, put you out of your misery."

"Shut up. You're an Ass." He said, as he passed out in the passenger seat.

They rode home in silence.

Tom spent the night. They left out early the next morning.

Mark had shaved his beard off and cut his hair.

"Well, you look a little better." Tom said, holding his own head.

"You look like Home Made shit." He replied.

"I'm gonna stop at the house and spruce up."

They met at the hospital. Mark was nervous.

He walked upstairs and saw Tom get off the second elevator.

"Hey." He said.

Tom showed his credentials to the guards, as they entered the room.

Tom pulled a small Zip-lock bag out of his pocket.

"Let me guess, Evidence?"

"Yes." Tom smiled sheepishly.

"This was all he had on him when he came in."

Mark opened the bag.

It was a set of numbers.

"What is it a code?"

"We don't know." He shook his head.

It said 914ORA.

"It doesn't match any coordinates."

"Let's go see the surveillance tape."

They were led to a small security station. The tape rolled.

You could tell it was snowing.

A few cars went by, then an ambulance.

Finally a large green Pick Up truck pulled up.

A man exited the driver's side door.

Once he came into the cameras view, mark could see his face. It was the kid.

Carl.

He opened the passenger door and pulled a large man out.

Mark knew it was grey by the shear size.

He dragged him near the door.

When the first set of glass doors opened, he startled, looking up.

He ran and jumped into the truck, and peeled out.

"It's the kid." Mark said.

"That's no kid," tom answered.

"He's CIA"

"Well whoever he is, he knows something. Rewind the tape."

The Guard rewound the tape. Mark watched it again, and again.

"There, stop the tape....now go back..foreward..."

When the truck pulled away, there was a slight reflection in the glass doors of the License plate.

It was a Wyoming plate.

He could make out the horse and rider, and 2 647.

There were two numbers missing.

Considering they had the description of the truck and a partial plate, it was huge lead.

"At least he brought him in." Tom said.

They had entered Grey's room again.

"I don't care if he's CIA, FBI, or mother Teresa, if I find out he had anything to do with Megan's death, I will kill him."

He was getting worked up now.

"I am going to kill anyone that hurt her, anyone that crimped a hair on her head, was involved, or even thought about it."

He spoke quietly now.

"But before that, I'm gonna hurt them, like they have never been hurt before.

I will rip everyone limb from limb till I find her."

Tom sighed. He knew better than to say anything.

The doctor walked in and broke the silence.

"Hello." He nodded.

Mark and Tom said hello.

Grey lay peacefully in the bed.

 "He came off the vent last week. Now it's just a matter of him waking up."

 Said the doctor.

"What are his chances?"

Mark asked.

"He seems to be making a good recovery. The last Ct scan showed no swelling. His gunshot wounds have healed. I predict a full recovery."

Mark walked over and touched Greys arm.

He leaned down, and whispered in his ear.

"Wake up you old son of a bitch, or I win. Besides I need your help."

They had a running bet since they had first met, as to who died first.

The loser would be left behind. But it had to be a heroic death.

 It was their code.

"This is an undignified death. It's not acceptable."

Mark visited Grey daily.

He read the paper to him, told him of recent news events, read the classifieds, and anything else he thought of to talk about.

The nurses liked the way he paced, around the room talking with his hands.

They often watched him through the glass.

Mark had renewed hope that Grey would know where Megan's body was so he could bring her home.

Every day, the nurses would turn and clean him and the physical therapy people came and exercised him.

It was Important so he didn't lose his muscle tone.

Sometimes Mark stayed for days.

The nurses had started bringing him a tray, and fresh coffee whenever they had it.

Usually at shift change.

The guard at the door continued.

It was after all a federal case now.

If he recovered they wanted him for a witness.

The night nurse was especially smitten with Mark.

Her name was Nancy.

She was 30, and had no children.

They became friends, and Mark shared some of the details with her.

She finally confessed that she liked him and he explained that he was flattered, but could not go there.

He apologized.

He explained that there would never be anyone in his life again.

That it would be disrespectful to Megan's memory.

They remained friends.

The days dragged on. There had been no luck on the license plate.

It had turned up stolen.

Mark and Nancy joked that he would soon be charged as a patient, if he didn't go home.

"I heard that people in coma can hear, that they just can't respond."

Nancy agreed that she had heard this too.

"Now here is a guy for you." Mark pointed to Grey.

"He's in coma, he doesn't talk back and doesn't make a mess."

"That's very sick." she told him.

"Seriously though, he's a good guy. He has a heart of gold, and I think he looks pretty good." Mark smiled. He was tired.

"The ladies have always liked him."

"I'm too young to date you son of a bitch."

The voice that came from the bed startled them both.

Mark walked over and smiled.

"It's good to see you man."

"Good to see you too. I've been listening to you drone on for weeks."

Grey was weak. He closed his eyes, and started to doze again.

"Is he ok? Is this normal?" Mark asked leaning over him.

"Yes, he's only sleeping now."

The doctor rushed in and checked him over.

"Well looks like he's going to be ok. All his vitals are normal. Give him a few days. He will be good as new."

Mark was glad, but he wanted to shake him awake and ask him about Megan.

He sat back down in the chair, and waited. He dozed on and off during the night.

The sun was just coming up. It would be over soon.

"Mark." He heard Grey say quietly.

He jumped up, and leaned over him.

"914 orange acre road Colin Nebraska……. The Kid is dirty."

He faded out again. Mark stood there for a moment.His heart was racing. This was it.

He was going to get Megan, and he was bringing hell with him.

He called Tom. They met in the parking lot of the hospital.

"Did you call the FBI?" Mark asked.

"No." their eyes and met and they both knew what it meant.

"I'm coming with you." Tom said

"Don't bring your conscience." Mark replied coldly.

They drove for four hours. Tom was unsettled.

Mark hadn't spoken a single word. He was deep in thought.

It was almost over.

He would bring her home and bury her. He could live with that.

They crossed into Nebraska. He stopped once to look at the map.

The street was easily found.

Mark parked across the street and waited until dark.

The house looked normal enough.

A white van was parked in the driveway.

Mark pulled the duffle bag out of the back seat.

The 40 caliber was already tucked into the holster under his jacket.

He stuck the 9mm in his pant's, and a bowie knife in his boot. It was pitch dark now.

There was no street light. Tom had taken care of that.

Mark stepped onto the small wooden porch.

Luckily it didn't creak under his feet.

He looked in the window.

There was a small television running, but no one in sight.

He signaled Tom, who headed around the back of the house.

His weapon drawn, Mark tried the door knob.

It turned in his hand.

He pushed it open and entered the house.

It was almost too easy.

The front door faced the back.

He saw Tom coming in the opposite door. A single lamp lit the dingy room.

Tattered blue curtains hung in the windows.

The paint was peeling off the walls, and the smell of mildew was overwhelming.

A painting of Anita hung on the wall. They definitely had the right place.

Mark looked up just in time to see the Albino come around the corner.

Tom almost ran into him.

Mark was large but the albino towered over him.

He grabbed Tom by the neck, lifting him clean into the air.

Mark shot him in the knee.

He went down on the other knee, but didn't loosen his grasp on Tom.

He aimed again and shot him in the shoulder.

The Albino dropped Tom onto the ground, and let out a blood curdling screech.

Tom rolled away and jumped to his feet.

Before they knew it the monstrosity was back on his feet again and heading straight for Mark.

He aimed again and shot him in the other shoulder.

Three men came from the basement door, guns drawn. Tom shot the first one in the neck.

The second clipped his Marks shoulder. Tom shot him between the eyes.

The albino ran out the back door, as the third man Knocked Mark to the ground.

He leaned down aiming his gun at his head.

Before the man knew it, Mark came up and plunged the bowie knife into his windpipe.

Carl came running out of the basement door with his hands up.

"Don't shoot, I'm CIA."

Mark snatched him by the neck and sat him at the small Dinette.

"Put your hands out where I can see them." He said.

Carl laid his hands face down on the table.

"Man, I'm glad to see you." He said.

Mark leaned in. "Don't talk unless I tell you to."

He was trying hard not to tear his throat out.

"Don't kill this one, we need information." Tom whispered to him.

"Where is Anita?" Tom asked.

Carl looked at mark.

"Answer him" Tom said.

"She left with some of the men last week, to rebuild the Cult. They went into Texas. There is a stronghold there."

"Where is Megan?"

"She is ...here." He said quietly.

Mark's heart sank. He still wasn't ready.

"How did she die." Mark was close to his face.

"She...Why are you asking me this?" he spat.

Mark stabbed the knife into his hand pinning him to the table.

Carl screamed. Mark tilted his head to the side.

"Take me to her." He said quietly.

Carl looked down at his hand, pinned to the table.

"Let's go." Mark said, ripping the knife back out of his hand, while Carl screamed again.

Tom followed them to the basement.

As they headed down the stairs the pungent smell of death and stagnant water hit them.

Mark was breathing hard now, trying to prepare himself.

He saw the freezers at the bottom of the steps.

Carl continued past them, to a second room.

It contained a small cell. Inside the cell there was a single cot.

There was a body on it, covered in a dirty blanket. Mark looked at Carl.

"Is this some kind of game you're playing?"

Carl pointed to a key hanging on the wall. "Cuff him to the cell." Mark said.

Tom reached in his back pocket and handcuffed Carl to the iron frame.

Mark unlocked the cell , while Tom Guarded the door.

It opened quietly. He was breathing hard now. The smell was overwhelming.

He walked over to the form lying on the cot. He slowly pulled the blanket off.

Megan lay there, with a small bundle in her arms.

He stood there like a stone. His feet rooted to the ground.

He saw her chest rise and fall.

Cooing noises were coming from the small bundle.

His legs felt heavy. He shook his head in disbelief.

He felt Tom move up next to him.

He leaned over and watched her breathing to make sure it was real.

Tears came to his eyes instantly. He looked up at Tom.

"She's alive." Mark reached down and touched her face.

She opened her eyes, and looked at him.

Megan smiled as a tear rolled down her face.

She reached her hand up to touch him.

When she came in contact with his face her eyes opened wide. "Are you real?"

"Yes babe, I am as real as it gets." He sobbed.

Tears flowed down her face. He pulled her into his arms, careful not to hurt the baby.

Megan closed her eyes and drifted off again. She was thin and very pale.

Mark pulled back the small blanket.

His son looked at him. Their eyes held. He laid her back, picked up the baby and handed him to Tom.

"No...I don't do babies. I don't..."

"Just take him, and don't you dare drop him."

He scooped Megan up and carried her past Carl, and out of the basement.

Tom followed close behind. He carried her to the Jeep.

"Let's get out of this shit hole." He said to Tom.

Megan opened her eyes as he strapped her into the backseat.

"They told me you were dead." She whispered, fading in and out.

"I'm not. I'm right here."

He took his son out of Tom's arms and hugged him to his chest, briefly.

"You want to wait for the ambulance?" Tom asked.

"Hell no, let's go. I don't want that freak coming back with reinforcements.

 I have to get them to the hospital."

 I don't trust anyone. I'll take my chances."

He formed a makeshift bundle with the blanket and strapped the baby into the back seat next to Megan, Waiting for Tom who had re-entered the house.

He came out with a stack of papers.

He had called the FBI.

 They were on their way.

"Let's get out of here. I'll wait for the boys in blue." Tom said.

They shook hands.

"I don't know how to thank you."

"Well you can start by not shooting my ear off next time."
He joked.

Mark looked at Toms bleeding ear. He must have nicked it
when he shot the Albino.

"Go on, get outta here, I'll catch up with you soon."

They shook hands.

Mark pulled out onto the road and headed for Wyoming.

Tears flowed down his face.

He took her to the nearest hospital and had her and the
baby checked out.

Both mom and baby got a clean bill of health, although
Megan was dehydrated and groggy.

Tom had since shown up and was staking the room out
personally.

The doctors deducted that Megan had been drugged with a
Sedation Drug, rendering her defenseless.

Once Mark spoke with the doctors, he sat down next to
Megan. The baby was in a small bassinet next to him. Tom
hadn't let them take him to the nursery. All baby checking
was to be done in the room, with either him or Mark
present.

With the Albino on the loose and Anita in the wind they
couldn't take any chances.

Mark held the baby and waited for Megan to wake up. She was getting IV fluids, and TPN, nutrition through a bag, into the IV.

She woke up briefly. "Where is my baby?"….

"He's right here." Mark said. Holding their son up where she could see him.

Tom had entered the room.

"Where is my baby?" She cried.

Mark held the baby closer. "He's here sweetheart, he's safe."

"No….I need to see my baby….." she looked at Mark.

"It's ok, honey."

"Where is my daughter?"

Mark and Tom looked at each other.

"What do you mean?" mark asked gently.

"I had twins."

Mark and Tom exchanged knowing glances.

"Babe, I swear to you on all that is holy, I will get our daughter back."